'I want to me... all!'

Shelley put a hand... her fingers were trembling. He only had to look at her to make her want to reach out and touch him. It was astonishing. She hated him, didn't she?

Christos spread his powerful arms, smiling, but without humour. The contained rage was very much in evidence.

'And here I am,' he announced softly. 'The very man you want.'

Dear Reader

Kalos orisate — welcome to Corfu. Although our Euromance series has already visited Athens and the Greek island of Crete, we thought you would also enjoy a trip to this fascinating island. Flower-carpeted and green, it captures the very essence of the Greek way of life, yet its bustling shops and night life make it a perfect spot for an unforgettable holiday.

The Editor

The author says:

'I fell in love with the Greek way of life on my first visit long ago. The elegant cafés of the Spianada in Kérkira are an enticement to while away the hours after a day at one of the many wonderful beaches close by. There are countless orchards of lemon, figs, grapes and kumquats, and round every curve is the ever-present turquoise of the Adriatic. The island is so magical that it makes the story of Calypso and Odysseus come alive. And Corfiot men must surely be descended from the Greek heroes of mythology! It is impossible not to fall in love with the people and the island.'

Sally Heywood

★ TURN TO THE BACK PAGES OF THIS BOOK FOR *WELCOME TO EUROPE*. . .OUR FASCINATING FACT-FILE ★

MASTER OF DESTINY

BY
SALLY HEYWOOD

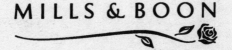

MILLS & BOON

MILLS & BOON LIMITED
ETON HOUSE, 18–24 PARADISE ROAD
RICHMOND, SURREY, TW9 1SR

First published in Great Britain 1994
by Mills & Boon Limited

© Sally Heywood 1994

Australian copyright 1994
Philippine copyright 1994
This edition 1994

ISBN 0 263 78491 6

Set in 10½ on 12 pt Linotron Times
01-9405-45483

Typeset in Great Britain by Centracet, Cambridge
Made and printed in Great Britain

CHAPTER ONE

IT WAS Christos. He was striding along the side of the dock towards the yacht. He was clad in denims, his faded blue shirt open just enough to reveal the black hair in its V, and the muscles of his chest strained against the rough cloth. He was older now, no longer a boy, his body more powerful than ever. He was coming for her.

Shelley found herself shrinking back against the bulkhead of her father's yacht in sudden fear. How she longed to go with him! But did she dare? Without pausing for further thought she grabbed a few clothes from the locker, stuffing them into the first bag she found, then raced back up the companionway.

Heart pounding, she threw a glance over her shoulder. There would be hell on board when Dad and Paula found she was gone. But she didn't care. He was here and that was all that mattered.

'Are you coming?' he called when he caught sight of her.

'Yes!' she whispered in panic. As she jumped down on to the quay she felt his arms reach out for her.

He pulled her against him and there was a long, dissolving moment before his mouth came down in powerful possession over her own.

* * *

She woke abruptly with a cry of longing on her lips. Her glance flew round the unfamiliar room. Where on earth was she?

Then it dawned. Of course, she was in Corfu.

Ever since Malcolm had told her she would have to come out here her sleep had been broken by dreams about Christos Kiriakis. Maybe it was her subconscious trying to tell her something. If so, it was wasted. She didn't want to have anything to do with him ever again.

Shelley blinked her eyes and tried to focus on what she had to do next. But the memories wouldn't release their hold. Time had passed — nine years, to be exact — and Christos probably didn't even live here now. It was long enough to have forgotten all about him. But she hadn't.

Haunted by the memory of his reckless good looks and the sound of his husky broken English, she flung herself out of bed. Standing under the shower, she wondered if he really had been as wonderful as she believed. At sixteen she had probably been far too impressionable.

A glance at her travel clock showed she would have to hurry if she was to catch the early morning ferry to Kassiópi.

The previous sleepless night showed up in thumbprints of tiredness beneath her eyes, but it couldn't detract from the prettiness of her oval face. Engagingly frank eyes of a striking amethyst-blue, together with a shining haze of soft blonde hair and a slender figure, gave her the classic looks that made heads turn.

Going to the window, she flung the shutters open

and saw the sun streaming down outside. It made the trees in the little square beneath look all gauzy and soft. A wild kitten trod delicately along the wall of the garden opposite, and she could hear the sound of splashing water from a fountain hidden deep in the lush green undergrowth beneath the palms. The early sun felt warm and inviting on her upturned face.

Tearing herself away, she hurriedly did her face, then extracted some summery linen shorts and a casual silk shirt from her travel bag. Slipping them on, she slid her feet into a pair of soft leather sandals, ran a brush through her blonde hair, then pulled on a cotton jacket. It was a shade of blue that complemented her delicate colouring to perfection. With the rest of her things still folded neatly in the bottom of her bag, she hurried downstairs to the foyer.

So much for my alarm call, she was thinking ruefully as she sped light-footed across the echoing marble tiles to the door.

A sleepy head emerged from Reception as Shelley reached the entrance. 'You go?' called a voice, bringing her to a stop. It was the proprietor's young son. When he saw his leggy blonde guest he gave an appreciative smile. 'I call cab.' He was already reaching for the phone.

She had settled up last night and informed Reception she had to make an early start. Now she shook her head. 'It's all right, thanks. I'll walk. It's not far to where the ferry boat leaves from, is it?'

'Where you wanna go?' asked the young man, coming round the side of the desk, eager to help.

He had a straight Greek nose like Christos and the same thick black hair and bronze skin, but he wasn't Christos and she didn't feel a tremor.

'I'm going up the coast as far as Kassiópi,' she told him, hitching her bag more comfortably on to her shoulder.

'Is quicker by car. I get for you.'

'No, it's all right, I've planned to arrive by sea. Somebody's meeting me at the port.'

'Is boyfriend?'

She shook her head. 'I'm here strictly on business.'

He picked up her bag. 'Here. Is heavy. I come with you. Show you short cut.'

As he was so keen to oblige she didn't argue. He led her briskly through a confusing network of half-familiar streets towards the sea front. She had walked here with Christos nine years ago, she was reminded. Firmly she forced him from her mind.

Her guide was leading the way at a fast pace, glancing at his watch and plunging further into the maze of streets.

Shelley would have liked to dawdle past the shops as there was an enticing array of boutiques, but there was obviously no time, and fortunately most still had their shutters down. She hurried on, getting a glimpse of a dress here, a pair of shoes there, while above them from the open windows of the apartments came the sound of families, voices echoing in high rooms or calling from the geranium-filled balconies that almost met across the streets.

Mingling with the aroma of fresh coffee and baking bread came the perfume of burning incense.

It wafted from the doorways of old Byzantine churches into the streets, and she could hear the frail sound of prayers from deep within.

This was Christos's territory, and she had a sudden terrifying feeling that round the next corner they would come face to face.

Keeping her head down, she followed her guide. 'These are called the *kandounia*,' he told her, indicating the marble pathways that wound between the walls of the tall Venetian houses with their peeling stucco. The paths were worn silver by the tread of countless passing feet over the centuries.

Christos and she had. . . Stop it! she scolded herself. Now her guide was leading her down some treacherously narrow steps, glimpses of the turquoise Adriatic showing in taunting little gaps between the white walls of the houses.

Then suddenly they were out on the broad sweep of Xenofondus Stratigou. Still carrying her bag, the boy led her triumphantly down the final stretch towards the ferry departure point.

When they reached the quay there was a crisp breeze blowing off the water. The ferry, with its white funnel, was just coming alongside. Her spirits rose at the sight; the busy harbour, the painted fishing boats, the lovely curve of the bay.

'Thanks for your help,' she said when they came to a halt. 'It was sweet of you to come so far.'

'You're welcome.' He shook hands and gave an appreciative smile. 'Have a pleasant journey. You come back, see me soon, yes?'

* * *

Smiling, Shelley watched him go, then joined the end of the queue waiting to board the ferry.

When Malcolm, chief executive in the London office of her father's property company, had asked her to come out to Corfu she had been hesitant at first, thinking of Christos and the last time she had been there.

'It's the most beautiful place,' she had told him, already deciding she would go. 'But I was a sixteen-year-old romantic in those days,' she had added with a smile. 'I'm sure it will seem quite different this time around.' She had laughed. 'Nowhere can live up to the fantasies of an adolescent girl high on poetry and Greek myth!'

Fully aware that she wasn't only referring to Corfu, she had wondered if Malcolm guessed what had made it so magical that first time.

He had said, 'I'll warn our site manager out there, Spyro Papandreou, to meet you at Kassiópi. He can take you out to the site. As soon as you've got everything back under control you could go back to Corfu Town to a decent hotel and take a few days' break. You'll have deserved it. I'll get you booked in somewhere really nice.'

'I could do with a holiday,' she'd agreed. 'Since Dad's been out of action the office has been like a mad house. Thank heavens things are slackening off now.' Then she had had an idea. 'Why don't I stay on site for a few days? I can stay in one of the villas and see if we need to make any changes. It'd be a useful piece of customer research.'

He had hesitated. 'I don't know whether that's a good idea.'

'But most of them must be near completion, ready for the season. What's to stop me?'

'That,' he'd said worriedly, 'is why you're going out there, isn't it? Shelley, don't count on being able to stay on site at all. Everything's way behind schedule.' His face had been sombre. 'I don't really know any more.' He'd given her a searching glance. 'You know I'd go out myself, but. . .'

'You can hardly leave the London end to run itself right now,' she agreed. 'Not with Dad breathing down our necks.'

They had both laughed and she'd added, 'Don't worry about me. I'll sort things out. I'm looking forward to the challenge!'

This was true. It meant she would be able to get her teeth into something on her own at last.

Just then the stern gate of the ferry began rattling down on its heavy chains, and it hit the quay with a loud crash. Immediately people started to pour off into the town, and the queue she was in started to shuffle forward with impatience. Soon they were all pushing and shoving their way on board with a lot of shouting, old ladies clad in black doing as much of it as anyone else.

Coming to Corfu was just the chance she had been waiting for, she told herself as she slowly pressed on up the steps to the upper decks. She longed to show her father what she could do. She felt it was about time he realised she was ready to handle more responsibility. She gave a shiver — at least, she hoped she was! If he intended to put her in charge of the European side of Burton's International one day he would have to let her do more. At present he

seemed to think she wasn't experienced enough,
even after three solid years in the London office
straight after college. Instead he had appointed
Malcolm Fitch.

Dear old Malcolm. In her heart she knew it was a
good appointment. He was very reliable and had
already spent ten years in the business. When her
father had had a heart attack recently it had been
Malcolm who had taken over, conferring on all
major issues with the bedridden Colin Burton, but
doing the day-to-day running himself from London.

Shelley managed to find a sheltered space in the
stern, and had just taken her seat when there was a
sudden resounding blast from the siren, and with a
lot of shouting the lines were cast off again. Slowly
the ferry edged from the quay.

She wound a white silk scarf round her head and
donned a pair of dark glasses. This was it. Pushing
up the sleeves of her blue jacket, she settled down
to enjoy the trip.

Kérkira, with its ancient Venetian fortress a grey
hulk on the horizon, was quickly left behind. The
wind got up, lifting the waves in little white curls.
The jagged coastline unfolded to their left and the
silky Ionian slithered through the channel between
the island and the mainland. She couldn't escape the
thought that now they were truly entering the king-
dom of Christos Kiriakis.

Putting a magazine up to her face, she decided to
keep him firmly out of her mind. But it wasn't so
easy.

What if their paths crossed? Would he remember
her after all this time? What would he be like now?

Unable to concentrate, she lowered her magazine. He would be in Athens by now. Being a success. Even at twenty he'd had the confidence of somebody who was going to make his mark.

Cross with herself for letting him back into her thoughts, she fixed her glance on the pretty coastline as they forged along. It would be a couple of hours before she was there. Then there was work to do.

She began to drift off, not quite asleep yet not fully awake.

After three weeks cruising the islands nine years ago, her hair had been a startling, dishevelled mane of silver. For some reason her appearance had upset Paula, her new stepmother. She had never lost an opportunity to criticise. They had sailed along this very coast and reached Kassiópi in mid-afternoon. It had been blazing hot. Shelley had been sunbathing on the top deck in a tiny pink bikini. To be frank, she had been bored, with no one of her own age to talk to. Paula and her father had been wrapped up in each other.

As they had entered the harbour disaster had struck. A trailing line had wrapped itself round the propeller shaft of their yacht. Her father had started to shout. All hell had seemed to break loose.

Then Christos had appeared, nineteen or twenty years old, driving his zippy little outboard motor boat to the rescue.

Wearing a pair of sawn-off denims, he had had a deep tan from working all summer in the marina. With his black hair and straight Greek nose, to Shelley, still in school, he had seemed the most romantic human she had ever seen. He had called up to them, then thrown his line over to their launch. She had caught it and their eyes met. He'd given her a rakish smile. Shelley had felt her life change course. Heavens, she had been so naïve!

After he had dived beneath the boat and freed the line he had given her a look of secret amusement, as if they'd shared something already—even though they hadn't exchanged a word. He had helped them find a berth in the busy marina, and afterwards, when her father had tried to push a bundle of drachma bills into his hand, he had shaken his head.

'No, is free.' His head had swivelled to where Shelley was leaning on the guard rail, and then he'd turned abruptly away, as if he'd found himself doing something he shouldn't. She'd watched him. He had gunned the engine of the small craft, circled their boat once as if reluctant to leave, then gone flying off into the thick of boats that filled the harbour.

She had thought she would never see him again. But she had. He'd come back. They had been together every day until that final humiliating showdown.

She shook herself awake. Here I am, daydreaming again, she scolded herself. The ferry nosed into another picturesque little harbour along the coast. Each time they docked she felt her senses sharpen, and then the tension ebb when they put to sea. Finally the ferry began to turn into Kassiópi.

Her hands gripped the rail as she gazed across the water and got her first glimpse of the place in nine years.

The harbour was sheltered by two headlands dotted with villas. The walls of a tenth-century castle straddled the hill just as she remembered, but there were a couple of hotels along the beach that were new. The stretch of water in front of the quay was busier than ever, with yachts and cabin cruisers and jostling caiques painted in all the colours of the rainbow. She noticed the familiar eye painted on the bows. Christos had told her it was to ward off evil spirits.

As the steamer entered it gave the traditional hoot on its horn to salute the icon of the Virgin donated long ago by a sea captain who had been saved from shipwreck on his way to Venice. Then they were coming alongside to the familiar shouting of the boatmen and the piercing whistle of the port customs official in his white uniform.

Eager to disembark, Shelley shouldered her bag and followed the crowd as it shuffled down the ramp. She stepped ashore with a feeling of curiosity.

Looking round, it was like stepping into the past. Things had changed in nine years, but not enough to spoil the charm of the place.

There was a small supermarket that was new, but the dairy where they had used to buy Greek yoghurt for breakfast every morning was still there, and so was the baker who had supplied them with warm, floury loaves and *baklavas* and *kataifi* running with Greek honey.

Then there was the hardware and camping store, still selling Calor gas and clothes-pegs and all the other hundred and one things the other shops didn't stock. But now there was a hairdresser's and an imposing glass and marble bank, and next to that a pretty white-painted boutique stocked with gold rings and bits of turquoise and lapis lazuli, and colourful silk scarves hanging in the doorway.

She forced her glance along the row of shops to the taverna at the other end. There were the same blue-painted wooden tables and chairs set haphazardly across the front, the same garden to one side. Then her tension ebbed. The name above the entrance was no longer Kiriakis but Georgiou.

More freely now she glanced up and down, hoping to see Spyro. He should have been here to meet her when the ferry docked. Sure enough, a car pulled up beside her. Her face broke into a warm smile. 'Spyro!' She went over to him. She had met him once in London, and now he got out of his car and clasped her hands firmly in both of his.

'Most happy to meet you again, Miss Burton,' he welcomed, brown eyes flashing their approval at her smiling face in its frame of soft blonde hair. 'I have strict instructions from my wife Anna to take you home at once for breakfast. You are to stay with us for as long as you like.' He picked up her bag and put it in his car.

'I hoped to be staying on site,' she told him. 'But Malcolm said it wouldn't be a good idea.'

He gave an apologetic frown. 'That's right. We have struck a major problem. Let's talk in the car.' He looked suddenly anxious and unhappy. 'Things are—how do you say?—problematical?' He gave a rueful shrug. 'I think you need the skill of a top diplomat to sort this out, Miss Burton.'

Her heart plunged. What if it was something she couldn't handle?

When they were safely in the car he gave her a

sideways glance, but seemed to find it difficult to start.

'Please go on, Spyro. What is it?' she prompted. 'Aren't the contractors reliable?'

He shook his head. 'It's not that. Everything goes wonderfully well in that way. But that almost makes it worse.' He frowned.

Shelley felt another flicker of alarm.

'It's down to clash of interests, Miss Burton. When your father was advised to buy this stretch of land he was very badly instructed.'

'Why, what's wrong with it?' she asked, quickly, imagining all kinds of disasters: landslides, inundation by the sea, crumbling foundations. But when she voiced these misgivings he gave a nervous laugh.

'Not quite that bad. It's to do with planning permissions for mains services and access. The thing is, Miss Burton, the new owner of the land adjoining our site refuses permission for power lines to run either over or under his land. What's more, he has blocked off our only access road. He claim we have no right to use it commercially.'

Her eyes widened. 'No right?' she exclaimed. 'But it's our own land. We can do what we like with it!'

'I'm only repeating what the other party are saying,' he apologised.

'But I thought that access road had been in use for years,' she puzzled. 'I remember looking at the plans myself.'

'It is true,' he agreed. 'But it led only to the original farm buildings on the peninsula. Now he claims the road is not intended for commercial use.'

'But can't we build a road round their plot and take in power lines from a different direction?'

'Unfortunately, no.' He shook his head. 'He owns everything to landward. It's possible we approach the site by ferry, but it is no good—too risky. The sea is very rough, with many rocks. That is why the beach remained undeveloped for so long.'

Shelley frowned. 'But, knowing Dad, I'm certain he would have checked all this a million times.'

'As I say, it's the new owner; he makes problems.' He spread his arms. 'It is like a game. Monopoly. Or maybe chess? We are checkmated.'

'I'd better go up right away and see what's what.' This was far more serious than she had expected. What if Dad found out? He would blow his top. As he was still convalescent, it could be fatal. Pushing the fear from her mind, she turned to Spyro.

His manner was even more agitated. 'What I'm trying to explain, Miss Burton. . .it is not possible to get on site. The contractors have been refused access for seven days now.'

'But this is ridiculous! You mean work has been brought to a complete standstill?'

He nodded and drummed nervously on the steering-wheel with his fingertips. 'There's a private security company there round the clock, a barrier across the access road. Believe me, it is the first time anything like this has ever happened. These people are under instruction to stop anyone—anyone,' he emphasised, 'from getting through.'

'We'll soon see about that!' She gave a determined lift of her small chin. 'I want you to take me down there straight away. Please, Spyro.' She touched his arm when he seemed to hesitate. 'I'll breakfast later.'

Reluctantly he put the key in the ignition.

'Have you managed to find out who's behind all this?' she queried as he slipped the car into gear. 'Obviously I'll have to set up a meeting with the company involved.' It must be one with money, backing, to employ full-time security people, she hazarded.

'It is some Athens-based company.' Spyro was unable to hide the disgust in his tone. As a true Corfiot, anyone or anything from the mainland was anathema to him. 'Called Monasco Holdings.' He made a gesture.

Shelley's pretty face became even more determined. 'Well, I'll go to Athens if need be.'

Spyro gave a half-smile. 'I admire your spirit, Miss Burton. But believe me, if I thought it would make any difference I would have gone to Athens myself. However, there is no need to go so far. The company has a base right here on Corfu—offices at a place in the hills called Villa Monasco.'

'Here?' Her blue eyes began to shine with renewed determination. 'Then what are we waiting for? Let's go and meet the boss of Monasco Holdings and get this whole thing sorted out!'

Her bravado abated a little when Spyro drove them out into one of the hidden valleys of Mount Pandokrator. Following the perimeter wall of a private estate, he eventually brought the car to a halt. A lodge guarded imposing entrance gates, now firmly shut. Through them she could see a drive

winding out of sight into the depths of the estate.
The feathery tops of palm trees were visible over the
wall. So this was the Villa Monasco. It was protected
like a fortress.

A uniformed guard stepped from the lodge, a
radio phone bulging in his hip pocket.

Shelley was just able to follow the gist of the
ensuing conversation between him and Spyro. It
didn't need Spyro's glum expression to confirm what
was said. It was no entry. By order.

She leaned forward and gave the guard a mega-
watt smile. 'I have business at the Villa with your
boss,' she told him in halting Greek, conscious that
what she said was probably quite ungrammatical as
well as untrue, but the guard looked as if he was
about to relent. First, though, he took out his phone,
jabbed in a number, and, after a brief word, spread
his arms in apology.

'I would say yes to you a million times, but my
boss, he say no.'

Spyro gunned the car with a muttered curse and
started to drive back down the valley. 'I was on the
phone all day yesterday trying to set up a meeting
for you, but "he's away" was all I got. "The boss
isn't here now".' He thumped the steering-wheel
with his fist.

Shelley had a sudden idea and gave him the order
to pull in by the side of the road.

'Look, this wall isn't very high, is it? I'm going in,
Spyro. I will get this matter sorted out. And to do
that I've got to meet the man in charge. Will you
wait for me?'

Without giving Spyro a chance to persuade her

out of her mad plan, she leapt from the car and ran through a plantation of palms towards a stretch of wall that was lower than the rest. Ignoring Spyro's half-hearted shout, she heard him cut the car engine as she reached it. A silence wrapped over her, broken only by the hammering of her own heart-beats as she scrambled to the top.

She sat astride the wall for a second, briefly regretting the damage it was doing to her linen shorts, then let herself down on the other side, landing with a thump on the baked earth. In another second she was pushing her way through some bushes deep into the grounds of the estate.

Easy-peasy, she was thinking as she rounded a scarlet bush of poinsettia. Then she stopped with an appreciative gasp. There, crowning the headland in front of her, was the villa itself.

It was magnificent. Flowering vines trailed in profusion over the parapet of a low white wall, and beyond that, with a spectacular view over the surrounding countryside, was the building itself. Geraniums and other more exotic plants splashed spots of colour at intervals along its wide terrace.

What a pity the owner seemed so unreasonable, she was thinking as she edged out from behind the poinsettias and began to make her way across a lawn towards the house. Amazed it was turning out to be so simple to get in, she expected at any minute to hear the shout of the irate owner. But nothing happened.

There didn't seem to be anybody around, and she began to wonder whether he was here after all.

A massive satellite dish sat at one end of the

terrace, big and ominous in the dazzling sunlight. She walked past it up some steps. This side of the villa was almost all windows made of black reflective glass. She peered into the nearest room, but was unable to make anything out. The shiny glass mirrored her own face back at her. Was there anybody on the other side? She tested the steel frame, wondering how the windows opened and where the nearest door was. There wasn't a sound.

Uneasy, she turned and looked back to the safety of the outer wall.

As she leaned against the widow, wondering what to do next, she felt a slight movement behind her. Then the window seemed to slide away. Before she could stop herself she found she was falling right inside the room.

'Welcome to the Villa Monasco,' intoned a voice directly above her head.

Still on her knees, she gazed up through a tangle of blonde hair. Whoever he was, he sounded furious, the deep male voice resonating with sarcasm. He was making it abundantly clear that she was anything but welcome. Knowing she was going to have to try to charm her way out of the situation, she struggled hastily to her feet.

A dark shape loomed over her, but after the dazzle of sunlight outside she couldn't focus properly.

Blinking, she felt her sight slowly adjust, so that she was just able to make out the shape of a man in a silver-grey suit. Angled down at her was a lean, darkly tanned face. Even before she managed to make out the separate features she recognised some-

thing forbidding in the arrogant line of his Greek
nose and the jut of a hard jaw.

Before she could bring a single word to her lips he
reached out a hand, his finely sculpted lips drawn
back in a parody of a welcome.

'*Kalimera, Shelley. Kalós írthate!*'

It was Christos.

CHAPTER TWO

CHRISTOS'S dark eyes lingered over her body, inching down the long, tanned legs, returning to dwell on her flushed features.

She flinched, feeling her self-possession ebb. 'I can't believe it's really you,' she blurted.

'Seeing is believing, Shelley.' He gave an arrogant jerk of his chiselled jaw.

She realised she was simply staring at him, too stunned to move. Pulling herself together, she became aware of several pairs of interested eyes focused on her, and when she jerked her glance round the room she realised she was standing in a large drawing office of some sort. Her confused glance picked out several display tables containing scale-models of buildings, the assistants frozen with lifted pencils at their drawing-boards, as if too astonished by her sudden appearance to move.

She dragged her glance back to Christos. He had changed since she had last seen him. No longer on the edge of manhood, he was now a fully mature male. But the black eyes were as hooded as on that last time she had seen him.

'You certainly lost no time,' he intoned, bringing her back to the present.

'What do you mean?' she managed.

'I mean I've had you on camera ever since you were turned away at the lodge.'

26

Something about being watched without knowing it sent shivers down her spine. He had actually watched her sauntering across the lawn, watched as she peered blindly through the smoked glass of this busy room? It was a sort of violation.

She raised stormy blue eyes to meet his glance. He was subjecting her to a penetrating appraisal that made the hair prickle on the nape of her neck in a flash of anger at what was possibly going through that labyrinth of a mind.

'I don't understand how you come to be here of all places.' She brushed a hand over her face.

The dark eyes angled down at her. He lifted both black brows.

'What do you imagine I'm doing here?' he intoned in a hard, flat voice. 'Did you expect me to be still working in the marina? Still running errands for the yacht charterers?' He gave a scornful bark of laughter. 'Time has moved on since those days.'

She flinched at his tone. To find him turned into a figure of such cold purpose was surprising, but to find him wearing such an aura of power was no surprise at all. But at the Villa Monasco? She was confused. He couldn't be in charge, could he?

'You'd better come along to my private suite.' Dark eyes flashed with some peremptory warning, as if he expected protests, but she felt only too relieved to leave the interested glances that trailed them to the door.

When it closed behind them they were alone. He gave a jerk of his black head. 'Come. Follow.'

He swivelled abruptly without allowing time for questions, and she had to hurry to keep up.

Aware of an ambience of pale luxury washing over her, she followed down one deeply carpeted corridor after another. When they reached the palatial suite with its dominant black desk that was evidently his centre of operations, he went to lean against the sill in the big bay on the opposite side of the room. He seemed thoroughly at ease, plainly master of the situation.

A nervous qualm ran through her. He was the embodiment of power and success, but intuition alerted her to the nuances of his mood. Astonished, she registered the presence of a deep inner rage beneath the urbane mask. It was like the last time she had seen him. His bleak regard then had concealed a towering rage, she remembered, and now she felt a primitive impulse to flee. But she had to resist. It was important to stand her ground. . . despite the crackling air enveloping them.

Taking a steadying breath, she waited for him to explain.

His black lashes flickered on the cruel prominence of his cheekbones, while something like a smile began to indent the corners of his hard mouth. 'So, you are here.' His glance inched over her flushed features. 'What do you want of me?' he asked softly.

Her spine stiffened. 'Want?' She tried to steady the sudden hammering of her pulses. 'I'm here on business, on behalf of my father's company,' she managed. 'I've been sent out here to get our beach project back on line. As you must know, Monasco Holdings is keeping our builders off the site. And I want to meet the man behind it all!'

She put a hand to her hair, and noticed her fingers

were trembling. He only had to look at her to make her long to reach out and touch him. It was astonishing. She hated him, didn't she? But time hadn't led her to exaggerate his impact, nor had it dulled her crazy desire for him.

She saw him spread his powerful arms. He smiled, but it was without humour, and the contained rage was very much in evidence.

'And here I am,' he announced softly. 'The very man you want.'

There was a challenge in the way his eyes glittered when he observed her involuntary reaction. Rightly or wrongly, she took his remark to be deliberately suggestive. It brought the angry flush back to her cheeks.

'You mean you're actually in charge here?'

'Very much so.'

She drew back.

Shocked to discover he was the man she was supposed to deal with, she heard her voice rise before she could check it. 'Surely you realise your actions could ruin us?'

He gave what seemed designed to pass for an apologetic shrug. 'Business is business, as I believe your father would agree. I really cannot allow access to the site. It would be too disturbing.'

'Disturbing? To whom? I know for a fact there are no houses for miles. That's a ridiculous objection!'

Anger ignited instantly within the black eyes. 'I have no intention of discussing the matter now. The guard at the lodge told you I was unavailable. Technically you're trespassing, and I would be within my rights to hand you over to the authorities. I don't like law-breakers.'

Somehow her glance fell, and she noticed his thigh muscles tense beneath the expensive suit, but she managed to drag her helpless gaze back to his face. He was watching her with a close, dark scrutiny that sent shivers through her.

Determined not to give in, she blurted, 'If *you* don't like law-breakers, *we* don't like cowboy companies cutting off access to our property! Those workmen cost money while they're standing idle.'

'Cowboy?' He looked mystified, then his brow darkened. 'Have you the nerve to contest the legitimacy of my company? I suggest you think twice before scattering your accusations around, Miss Burton. Even in this "backwater of civilisation", as your stepmother was pleased to call it, we have a legal system. And, I may tell you, slander is a punishable offence.'

'This is ridiculous,' she defended. 'Your company barricades us off our own land, then you have the gall to accuse us of breaking the law! I'd like to know what law says you can put barricades all over the place!'

Lifting her small but very determined chin, she continued, 'I shall be most surprised to discover you have acted legally. Let me say I intend to take professional advice as soon as I leave here.'

There, that's told him, she thought. Her lips were trembling and she couldn't get any more words out.

His black eyes glinted, observing her flushed face with apparent derision. 'You intend to make a fight of it, then?'

She nodded, too angry to speak, fists clenching out of sight behind her back.

'So now we know where we stand?' He gave an easy chuckle, blatantly expressing contempt for her threats.

Unnerved by the black eyes, she gabbled, 'Monasco have known for ages a representative from Burton's wanted to discuss matters. Yet even a simple request by our chief executive in London to talk over the phone has been refused. It's clear it was due to sheer bloody-mindedness. I've been forced to come out here myself to try and sort things out. Your reluctance to talk can only mean you know you're in the wrong and want to delay matters for as long as possible. There can be no other explanation.'

'Can't there?' His lips twisted, and both black brows lifted a fraction.

He moved his muscular body from beside the window. 'We're going to talk.' He managed to make it sound like a threat. He glanced at a gold band on his wrist. 'But it won't be now. I flew in from Hong Kong less than an hour ago. My assistant was quite right when he told you I was unavailable. I was just about to take a shower and get changed. This is not a convenient time to indulge ourselves in discussing what amounts to a *fait accompli*.'

'It's deliberate sabotage, Mr Kiriakis! I suggest you get ready to hear from our solicitors!'

Too angry to listen to any more, she moved to the door, but then she felt him move across the room towards her. From behind, his voice sounded like silk in her ear. 'Surely having gone to the trouble to break in, you're not now going to break out?'

Trembling, her hand tightened on the doorknob. She felt his hand close warmly over her own. He pressed the door shut, and with it her chance of escape.

She twisted her head, trying to cut off all feeling where she was branded by his touch. 'I shan't have to break out, shall I? I'm not a prisoner,' she croaked. Unable to meet his glance, she felt him angle his head so that he could look down into her face.

Helplessly her eyes lifted and their glances meshed. She felt her lips tingle and part. Transfixed, she could only stare at him. Nothing seemed to separate them. His force made the air electric around them.

His effect on her must be obvious, she thought furiously, because he gave a rasp of amusement, stepping back to make a show of releasing her.

'Not a prisoner. Don't be afraid.' He moved into the middle of the room. 'I am not a barbarian.' His black glance found hers and held it, and she knew instantly that he was remembering the accusations levelled at him by her stepmother.

His black eyes raked her features. 'I intended to arrange a more convenient meeting, but you know what they say about the best laid plans. Now you've forced your way in here you'd better sit down and listen.'

Appalled at the effect he was having on her usually controllable emotions, she took an incautious step towards him. 'Listen? No, I think I've done enough listening! You listen to me,' she countered breathlessly. 'Discussion isn't going to change anything. Action will. Every extra day's delay costs us money. As soon as the men are back at work I'll be on the next flight to London. There'll be no need to waste your valuable time in discussions.'

One look at his face was enough to show the effect of her words. He seemed barely able to control his feelings. A muscle jumped at the corner of his mouth with the effort.

He began to prowl towards her in silence. She felt herself shaking at finding herself the focus of such raw anger. As he advanced she became aware she was shrinking back against the door, expecting to be torn to shreds for her audacity.

But he didn't touch her. It seemed he hadn't intended to. He merely reached past her to a phone on the wall. His face was white. 'We'll have coffee,' he clipped. 'Don't argue.'

He spoke to somebody in another part of the villa in his deep, rich Greek voice, and after he replaced the receiver he slanted her a hard glance. His jaw was clenched, the muscle near his mouth still hinting at the strength of the emotion he controlled.

She mustn't let this opportunity slip. If only her knees would stop trembling! She couldn't put two coherent thoughts together with him glowering at her like this.

She raised her head. 'It was a shock coming face to face with you just now,' she admitted candidly. Her lips trembled. 'You don't seem at all surprised to see me. Did you guess the Burton's you were dealing with was my father's company?'

He gave her an ambiguous up-and-down glance, his black eyes unfathomable, emotions now apparently under control. His answer was oblique. 'I always know with whom I am doing business.'

She bit back any comment on this infuriating reply. 'It's quite a coincidence,' she asserted.

His controlled stillness made her feel like a gibbering idiot. She felt worse when he gave a derisive lift of the black brows. 'Coincidence?' He weighed her expression then gave a harsh laugh. Just then one of his assistants poked his head round the dividing doors. He was followed by a young woman bringing in the coffee.

Christos had obviously got a very tight schedule. While she fumed and sipped her coffee he dealt with half a dozen urgent matters in his incisive Greek.

She moved over towards the window, where she could watch him.

The miracle was that he had remembered her at all. He even remembered Paula calling him a barbarian. Her remark had obviously rankled. In fact Paula had yelled a lot of really horrible things at him in the midst of that last awful scene, most of which Shelley prayed he had not understood.

Now he was rapping out instructions to someone on the phone, and she was doubly impressed when he suddenly switched to fluent French. Nine years ago he had spoken a sexy brand of broken English. It had been enough to deal with the yacht owners who berthed in the marina, and he had picked up smatterings of Dutch, German and French too, all of them limited though colourful. Discovering how well he spoke both English and French now, she wasn't surprised he was such a raging success. That had been one of his attractions: his energy; the magic of knowing he could make things happen.

He happened to raise his glance from the sheaf of papers he had been poring over. Their eyes met. He gave a sudden smile and came over to her, quoting in a derisive tone, '"Coincidence"? My dear Shelley, do you really believe that?'

His aides took the papers back into the next room. 'What is strange,' he continued more harshly, 'is the ease with which your boss allowed you to come out here alone. I expected you to have an escort. I'm sure your father wouldn't allow you to gallivant around Europe like this. He was over-protective if anything.'

'My boss?' she queried, flinching at the chill in his tone.

'Fitch,' he rapped. 'Wasn't he put in charge six months ago?'

She nodded.

'And how long do you think he will survive against your father? He's already put his job on the line by letting you come out here alone.'

Stung to defend Malcolm's judgement, she retorted, 'Fitch, as you call him, knows I can look after myself. And besides, I wanted to come out.' She tried to change the subject. 'How did you know he was my boss?'

'You mean you can twist him round your little finger?' he interjected, ignoring her question.

Their eyes met and she laughed edgily, saying, 'He treats me as a fully adult working colleague, not a porcelain doll. Besides,' she continued, 'I'm in constant touch with Head Office. If I don't report in regularly there'll be trouble. Dad would see to that.'

'But how much can he know from far-away St Lucia?'

Shelley felt her jaw drop. Recovering quickly, she said defensively, 'You have done your homework, Mr Kiriakis.'

'I find it pays,' he rejoined drily.

Registering her reaction, he curved his lips in a mirthless smile. 'Your welfare used to be such an issue for him in the old days, demanding I bring you back to the yacht not a minute late. Though these days — ' he smiled without humour ' — I gather he's giving everything away.'

She frowned. 'Not at all. He's been extremely ill.'

'But his business is effectively in the hands of Fitch,' he countered disparagingly.

'You seem to be very concerned about Malcolm for some reason. He happens to be a well respected and popular executive,' she defended with spirit. 'And, contrary to what you seem to think, Dad is still very much in control.' She tried to give a light laugh to show she wasn't shaken by just how much he knew about the internal running of Burton's. 'In fact he never changes,' she continued. 'He's still breathing down our necks.'

'Not at the moment he isn't. You're trying to run London yourselves.'

Shelley felt confused by his criticism of poor old Malcolm. Her glance flew round the beautiful room, and a sense of its remoteness filled her. Her confidence faltered.

He was called to one of the phones yet again, and

she fumed at being pushed to the back of the queue once more. As the minues ticked by she kept remembering the empty building site and the expensive equipment lying idle. It was like watching money melting away.

Christos seemed to be treating it as a game, and it would have helped if she knew what stakes they were playing for. Why was it such an important issue for him? What would he gain by winning? It didn't make sense.

When he eventually turned back her nerves were wound tight, and something about the detached way his glance swept over her made them finally snap. 'You're doing this deliberately!' she accused. 'It's sheer bloody-mindedness. You obviously hope to do a deal of some sort. So tell me about it. I demand to know your terms!'

She came to a halt. He was simply staring at her.

Going to take up a position in a leather chair behind the impressive black desk, he allowed his glance to trickle frostily over her dishevelled form. His cold glance took in her naked legs, her tousled hair, the now somewhat crumpled blouse. Then his cut-glass accent began methodically to rip her to shreds.

'What an extraordinary girl you are,' he began, taking his time and speaking in a voice as devoid of feeling as permafrost. 'Plainly this little setback is the be-all and end-all of your concerns at present. I have many other matters than this on my mind, as you can see.' He eased the tension in his broad shoulders. 'You break in to my grounds, attempt to force an entry into my headquarters, then have the nerve to start hectoring me to do this and do that as if I'm some office boy on your father's pay-roll.'

He gave a harsh laugh. 'You have much to learn, Miss Burton.' He narrowed his glance. 'First you must learn good manners. You are a guest in my country and cannot throw your weight around as if you own the place. Second, you must adapt yourself to other ways of doing business — less frenetic ways, perhaps, but no less effective than the way you're familiar with. And third,' he went on relentlessly, 'you really must do something about your appearance. It is quite distracting to see you looking so *distraite*.'

Shelley gasped. A red flush crept over her skin. She backed to the door. Her fingers grappled for the handle. 'If that's all you have to say, then I may as well leave,' she muttered hoarsely. She dared not trust herself to say more.

Pressing her shoulder against the door, she found herself standing outside in the corridor. With an effort she forced her limbs into action and groped her way in the direction of what she prayed was the exit. To hell with him, she was thinking, mind seething with the insults she'd like to hurl at his head. Yet she was confused by a niggling feeling that he might be right.

She had behaved abominably, barging in and trying to force the issue like that, demanding to hear his terms in that insulting way. What if it hadn't occurred to him to do a deal?

But in justification she was worried to death about how her father was going to react when he heard his dream village was in jeopardy. She had to get things moving again. She simply had to.

To hell with Christos Kiriakis, she repeated under her breath as she hurried along. I hate him, I hate him. He won't win! He can't win!

The sound of a door opening behind her made her increase her speed. He caught up with her before she'd gone far.

He didn't try to make her stay. She watched him turn to a door into another room and there was a brief glimpse of a bank of security TV screens before the door clapped shut. When he reappeared a moment later a jeep was already driving on to the forecourt. 'Get in. He'll drive you down to the lodge.'

Blindly she allowed him to open the glass doors and escort her down the steps. She was powerless to utter a word of apology or even to defend her actions.

As she climbed in he asked, 'Where can I contact you?'

'I'm staying with my father's site manager,' she muttered, desperately ashamed, but unable to say anything to rectify matters.

'With Spyro?'

She nodded.

'I know how to find him.'

Of course you would; you know everything, she thought furiously, only just managing to hold the words back in time.

He gave a curt nod. 'I'll be in touch.'

With an abrupt '*Adio*' he swivelled and made his

way rapidly back up the steps. Then he was lost to sight inside the building.

A few seconds later she was deposited outside the lodge gates, the jeep disappeared, and the guard leaned out through the window of the lodge, giving her a wave as she began the long trudge to where Spyro had parked the car.

CHAPTER THREE

'WELL?' demanded Spyro with a worried frown the minute she slid in beside him. 'What happened?'

'I managed to get into the villa and meet the man behind all this.' She paused and gave a rueful shrug. 'I feel as if I've been mauled by a tiger. He's called Christos Kiriakis.'

The beginnings of a sympathetic smile were wiped from Spyro's features in an instant. 'Who?' Brown eyes probed her face in astonishment.

'What's wrong?' she exclaimed.

Spyro looked heavenwards, then dramatically closed his lids before giving a defeated shake of the head. 'I know this man. He was in my class at school.'

Turning to give a glance at Shelley's surprised blue eyes, he went on, 'He left as soon as he could to start a business of his own in the marina. He ran it through summer, and worked on a building site in the winter. He was hard as nails. Very dynamic. Always one to call the shots. Like his father. Both very correct, very hard. His father was a big man in the wine trade. He also owned the restaurant on the waterfront.'

He paused and seemed to give the matter some thought. 'That must be until nine, ten years ago. Then something happened. . . Christos disappeared. I lost track of him.'

41

Shelley kept silent. She knew about Mr Kiriakis owning the taverna and Christos's job at the marina; the rest of what Spyro had told her was new.

'Well,' she said, at a loss as to what to say next, 'I don't know what we're going to do now.'

Spyro frowned. 'Nobody has seen him in Kassiópi, otherwise I would have heard. He can't have had the villa long. I knew work was going on out there, but didn't connect it with him. It's years since I gave Christos Kiriakis a passing thought.'

He looked closely into her face. 'So what did he say to you?'

Shelley felt uncomfortable. 'He said a lot of things,' she mumbled. 'But the main thing is, nothing will make him change his mind about access to the peninsula.'

'Damn him. . .! Forgive me, Miss Burton,' he corrected hastily, remembering who she was.

'It's all right, Spyro. Secretly I've been saying worse than that since I came face to face with him! And,' she went on, 'why not call me Shelley, since we're allies in all this?'

Spyro touched her on the arm. 'Listen, then, Shelley, don't worry. I know this project is important for your father. I've worked for him for five years and I find him a very decent and plain-speaking fellow. It breaks my heart to fail him on this, especially as he is not in wonderful health.'

'With your help we won't fail,' she affirmed. 'But we mustn't tell Dad yet. He would only worry. We'll sort something out first. We're not beaten yet!'

As he drove back towards Kassiópi she told him that Christos had asked where she was staying so he could arrange another meeting. 'Probably so he can take further pleasure in refusing us access,' she commented angrily. 'But I'll do my damnedest to make him see reason.'

Spyro's wife Anna was a short, dark, bustling woman in her early thirties with a quick, humorous quirk of the mouth that showed her lack of reverence for pomposity. There was a gaggle of children clinging to her skirts when she came to the door, and she was wiping her hands on her apron as she said, 'I expect you an hour ago!' She smiled. 'Is everything all right?'

Spyro gave a grimace. 'Show Miss Burton up to her room, Anna, while I take the car round the back.' His eyes lit up as they met his wife's, and she opened the blue-painted door of their village house wider and, still smiling, invited Shelley into the shadowy entrance hall. There was a smell of wild thyme and soap and, faintly, the aroma of coffee filtering up from some inner recess of the building.

After telling Shelley to leave her bag in the hall for Spyro to fetch, Anna led the way upstairs, trailing her fingers over the highly polished mahogany banister to steady herself. She indicated the bulge beneath the black cotton shift she wore. 'He takes my breath already!' She smiled with the contentment of a happily pregnant woman, and observed with a brief glance at Shelley's wedding finger, 'No children.'

'No husband.' Shelley smiled. 'And that's the way I like it!'

Anna gave a disbelieving smile. 'Have you come straight from London, travelling overnight?'

Shelley shook her head. 'No, I spent one night in Corfu Town. I arrived too late yesterday to come straight up here.'

'Ah, Kérkira. Is it busy yet?'

Shelley shook her head again. 'Not yet. But I expect things will be frantic over Easter.'

Anna nodded. 'Tourists.' She smiled. 'All holidays. Everyone on holiday. Good for Burton's International; good for Spyro and me, yes?'

'Very good!' Shelley agreed, carefully avoiding the reason for her visit. She wouldn't have discussed business with Anna anyway, but doubted too whether her English would have been up to it. The other woman took her by the arm. 'I show you your room. My favourite. Come.' She went across the landing and opened a door into a room at the back of the house, and invited Shelley to go inside.

'Oh, this is so pretty! You are kind to put me up!' Shelley's exclamation was full of genuine delight, and she pushed her worries briefly to one side, eyes sparkling as they swept the pin-bright room. It was light and sunny with white-painted furniture and a crisp blue and white bedspread.

She made her way over to the French windows. They opened on to a small balcony, and, stepping outside, she gazed beyond a few jumbled rooftops to a glimpse of the sea. It was so blue that it hurt the eyes after the wintry grey of London, and glittered in the early morning sunshine. A few yachts were already out.

'It's wonderful!' she repeated, leaning out to look

at the view, thoughts swamped for a moment by sudden memory. 'It's exactly as it was.'

She wished she had been more guarded. Anna immediately wanted to know when she had been here before, where she had stayed, and who with, and she had to say hurriedly, 'Oh, it was years ago, Anna, when I was still at school. I was with my parents on our yacht. We were doing the islands. Dad was looking for property to buy. That's when he acquired the apartments down town.'

'Mimosa Holiday Apartments? Yes, very pretty. Been there a long time.'

Shelley nodded. 'We never went anywhere without Dad using it as an opportunity to expand. I don't think he's ever had a simple holiday in his life!'

Shelley could hear the children calling now deep inside the house, as Anna, after a promise of a cup of coffee, went downstairs. As soon as the door closed she sank on to the bed and kicked off her sandals. She would have to change into clean clothes, though Anna hadn't so much as raised an eyebrow at her so-called '*distraite*' appearance!

She gave a hugh sigh and stretched out on the bed. It was strange to be here. It was oddly exciting, despite the humiliating encounter with Christos. As soon as she had sorted out the problem over access — she grimaced — she would have a few days to herself, as Malcolm had advised. He would have to be called at some point and put in the picture.

As she had promised, Anna provided a pot of fresh coffee with some warm rolls and a dish of runny Greek honey. By the time Shelley emerged a few minutes later, they were set out on a table under the clematis-hung trellis at the back of the house. Sunlight filtered through the tracery of green leaves that would thicken and darken to provide welcome shade as summer approached.

Now, in the early days of April, the air was like wine cooled from the cellar, only the sunlight filtering through the canopy above her head hinting at the sort of day that lay ahead. Shelley moved her chair into a buttery patch of sunlight, shrugging her jacket from her shoulders in order to make the most of the warming rays.

It was very peaceful here, with the sound of the children's voices among the trees.

Remembering Malcolm, she got up and went to the kitchen window. 'Anna!' she called inside. 'I have to ring London. May I use the phone?'

Spyro came up behind Anna with his arms round her waist, and poked his head out beside hers. He worked from home, and there was a properly equipped office on the ground floor. 'There is a phone in my office, Shelley. Treat the place as your own. I've cleared a space for you.'

Malcolm was on the other line when she eventually got through, and, somewhat relieved, she left a message with Gwen, his secretary, to tell him simply that she had arrived safely and would be in touch.

She went upstairs to get her briefcase with notebook and pen, and rummaged to the bottom of her holdall to find her camera as well. It would be a good idea to get photos of the security block on the access road. If the matter came to court, as it very well might, it would all be evidence. She ran a quick shower, changed into a skirt and a dark blue T-shirt, pushed a comb through her hair, then snatched up her things and went down.

'I'd like to go out to have a look at this barricade with my own eyes,' she told Spyro.

He had a couple of children draped about his person but started to disentangle himself when he heard what she intended. 'OK. Let's go.'

She caught one of the children up and deposited him back in Spyro's surprised arms. 'You needn't bother to come. If it's as you say, I won't get near the place. You've seen it. But I just want to have a look for myself from a distance. Pointless both of us going down.'

'Then you must take my car.'

'What if you suddenly find you need it? No, I'll hire one. Can you fix that for me?'

'No problem.' Still draped in assorted offspring, he hobbled through into the office and she heard him on the phone.

Back in a moment, he announced, 'Andreas will have one ready for you in five minutes.' Insisting on doing a little drawing to show her how to get to the side-street where the garage was, he came with her to the door. 'If you can't find it, anybody will direct you. And——' he paused '—be careful down there.'

Assuring him she was always careful, and only glad he hadn't seen her performance earlier that morning, in a minute or two she was walking briskly down towards the square. She was smiling to herself. Life out here lacked the edge it had in London. But she rather liked it. There was something charming about doing business in a house full of little children. It made it all more human. Anna was lucky, she concluded. She had a husband who obviously adored her and that pretty house, smart as a new pin, full of life and love.

I'm getting broody in my old age, she observed wryly as she reached the corner of the street marked on Spyro's map.

Hiring the car was done quickly by Greek standards. She drove it down the cobbled street into the square to pick up the main road out of town. It was market day, and she had to drive at a snail's pace until she was clear. Once out of town she rolled down the windows and began to enjoy the drive.

The road drifted pleasantly between the sea and the mountains, sometimes dipping down between plantations of olives, at others skirting the edge of lemon groves and innumerable empty beaches. Only when it started to climb did the orchards give way to scrubby hills strewn with rocks, and she guessed she was nearing her destination at last.

There was supposed to be a last long climb to the summit of a hill, then the plain stretching to the peninsula would be visible. The car laboured up to the top, then she gave a sigh of satisfaction. This was it. Below lay the narrow track dwindling on towards the cliffs. And there — yes, she could see it now — was an old shepherd's hut and a coil of barbed wire stretching from one side of the narrow road to the other.

Although it was expected, the sight of it made her cheeks flame. How dared he do this? Presumably the scrubby, unfarmable territory on both sides belonged to Christos. It was fit for nothing but sheep and goats by the look of it, so why was he refusing permission to cross? What harm could they do? It was sheer bloody-mindedness, she surmised. A deliberate show of power.

Climbing out of the car, she dragged her camera from its bag and peered through the viewfinder. There was a movement down below, and she guessed she'd been spotted. Tough, she thought. Let him inform Mr Kiriakis he's under surveillance! She took a few snaps, then turned back towards the car.

She found the scene rather desolate. There was something sinister in its isolation from the rest of the island.

No wonder it had never been developed. Their own patch was much the same. It had taken someone with vision, like her father, to see its potential and have the will to make something of it.

She climbed into the car and sat for a few minutes with her eyes closed. The last twenty-four hours were beginning to catch up with her. She decided she'd better be getting back.

Drowsily reaching for the ignition key, she heard a sound in the distance. It was growing louder and clearer and was undoubtedly a car being driven at speed along the single-lane track. She couldn't turn her own car until the other vehicle had passed, so she sat where she was to wait.

Her head swivelled when she heard it screech to a stop. A cloud of yellow dust billowed around it before settling theatrically over the motionless vehicle.

It was a white Range Rover. She became aware of a man swinging down from the other side. It was a tanned figure in denims. He was alone. He came round the bonnet. It was Christos.

Automatically she clicked the lock on her door.

'I knew you wouldn't be able to resist a look,' he mocked, coming over to the hire-car and resting his arms with insulting familiarity on the windowsill before she could shut it. 'Seen all you want to see?'

She gave him a hard look. 'Obviously not.'

Her sarcasm wasn't lost on him. He gave a pleasant laugh. 'And your mood hasn't improved either.'

She glowered. 'You told me you were too busy to talk. Yet here you are dogging my footsteps as if you've nothing better to do.'

'Things moved faster than expected this morning.' He swung back towards his own vehicle before she could ask him to explain, calling over his shoulder, 'Follow me.'

She watched him swing up into the driver's seat, then the Rover was bumping away down the track towards the barricade. He was almost at the bottom of the hill by the time she could bring herself to let off the handbrake. Who the hell did he think he was? His peremptory manner really made her hackles rise.

It had been the same before when he had used to call for her at the yacht. He had used to stand on the pontoon, big and bronzed and gorgeous in a disreputable pair of cut-off denims and some scuffed trainers, his dark eyes challenging hers.

Scrambling down the gangplank like an eager puppy, she had followed him at once.

Now here she was, doing it again!

Gritting her teeth, she allowed the car to coast

down the slope until the gears meshed, then she let it crawl after him, reduced to a snail's pace by the fact that he had wound down his window and was carrying on a cheerful conversation with the old man who was posted in the hut. The old fellow was keeping pace with the moving vehicle, one hand resting against the wing, and she saw him rap it good-naturedly as Christos increased speed. When she drew level he gave her a toothless smile, waving her past.

He obviously ate out of Christos's hand, she adjudged, nodding to him, scarcely able to bring a smile to her lips.

Christos drew to a halt further on and came striding back towards her. 'You'd better leave your car here. The track isn't too good. Come.'

Yes, sir, no, sir, she thought rebelliously. But it obviously made sense to travel on in the more robust vehicle.

Reluctantly she followed him and climbed in beside him. She felt horribly aware of him as the Range Rover lurched from side to side over the ruts, throwing them against each other, making her conscious of every brush of his arm against her own. As soon as they bucked to a stop in the compound she wrenched open the door and jumped down.

Her spirits plunged as she looked round. Appalled, she took in the sight of half-built villas round what should have been the main square of the beach club. In the middle was a fountain, dry and full of builder's debris. The retail units, the restaurants, all the many buildings whose foundations had already been laid, had their iron re-bars sticking up into the air like broken bones. She felt like crying.

This was to have been her father's dream place. Now it looked like a bomb site, no sign of life, just half-finished shells open to the skies. He had had such plans for it, wanting to build a real summer community, proudly showing her the designs for it from the very beginning. Later he had discussed it at every stage, welcoming her suggestions and making her feel she was a real part of the team. They had discussed the detailing of the interiors, planned the fitted kitchens and bathrooms, and made sure every unit had its own sun-terrace and pool and the details that would make each villa unique. He had even had tiles specially commissioned from a top designer, based on a local Venetian pattern.

Oh, Dad. . . She closed her eyes. Thank heavens you can't see any of this!

Remembering whose fault it was, she turned her blazing eyes on Christos. 'Well, I hope you're pleased with yourself! This amounts to nothing less than vandalism!'

He had the nerve to laugh outright. 'Hardly, my dear. I'm not destroying anything.'

'No?' She stared round helplessly, almost too upset to speak. Eventually in a low voice she announced, 'You're destroying one man's vision of paradise. That's vandalism, Mr Kiriakis.' She swivelled when he came up beside her. 'Don't you dare touch me!' she exclaimed, though he hadn't raised a hand. Hot waves of emotion flared over her flesh as she imagined his fingers trailing over her naked skin. She backed away.

'I've been telling myself all morning things aren't as bad as I believed,' she managed to croak. 'But I was wrong. All Dad's wonderful ideas have been turned to dust!'

'Don't over-dramatise. It's not as bad as that. At least the foundations haven't been dug up.'

'You wouldn't dare. . .!' She gave him an astounded glance, but he was only trying to wind her up, and started to laugh softly as he walked away.

As she followed she noticed the top soil blown in mounds against the walls, the silt-drifted pools, the shutterless windows, the roofless shells of what were supposed to be luxury villas. A grand opening had been planned in a couple of months' time to coincide with her father's sixtieth birthday. Now there was no hope of completing on time.

'How could you do this?' She caught his sleeve. 'Why, Christos? Look at it!'

She released him and ran forward, peering into one villa after another, observing the unclad concrete floors and the rough, unfinished brickwork. A lizard, startled by her appearance, scuttled across one corner, and she drew back with a cry.

Tears stung her eyes, tears of anger, of impotence, of something like grief that the man she had once worshipped could be the instrument of such desolation.

She jerked round as he came up behind her.

His brooding glance alighted on the perfect oval of her face and lingered there.

Then she felt something deep in his eyes catch

hold of something inside her own, and she put up a hand as if to ward it off. 'Tell me why you're doing this,' she breathed raggedly, scarcely conscious of the space separating them. 'Why destroy everything? What purpose does it serve?'

There was a moment of stillness. Far away she could hear the song of cicadas. The breeze drifted the warm scent of flowers their way. Somehow she felt she had to get away from him, and retreated further into one of the empty buildings. He followed her, coming to a stop in the gap where a door should have been, his back against the sun.

He lifted one hand towards her, reaching out and slowly bringing his fingers to her hair. She felt them slip among the blonde strands. Then his touch was like a feather against her cheek. A million atoms of desire began to propel her towards his arms as she saw him open them and reach out for her, and then his power was sweeping over her and he was crushing her against his chest.

Her head tilted in a wild mix of surrender and rebellion, and a hoarse rasp of sound dragged from her throat as his lips came down.

It was a sweet and savage plundering of her lips, a touching and tasting as of something precious and rare, then the desire began to build and his mouth began to search hers with a deepening hunger. She felt his hands travel up underneath her T-shirt and begin to mould her heating flesh, locking her against his hard arousal as his mouth ranged down the side of her neck, desire running like hot flame beneath her skin.

And then she knew this was what she had always wanted. This man. With this black energy.

Through all the years this was the man she had longed for. Loving him had changed her life. Now, again, he held her happiness in the palm of his hand.

But, as before, it meant nothing to him.

CHAPTER FOUR

CHRISTOS released her as quickly as he had taken her. With his back against the light she couldn't make out his features. But she felt his black will focus unwaveringly on her. Then she saw his shoulders strain with a sudden release of energy before he pivoted and began to make his way back towards the square without a word.

Her knuckles scraped against the raw brick of the wall she had bumped up against, and a hot rage rose thickly up her body at the casual way he had taken then discarded her.

Could he tell what havoc his kiss had aroused? She prayed not. The humiliation of knowing he could make her feel like this, despite everything, was horrible enough in itself without the added gall of having him know it.

She ran after him. 'Does it give you perverse pleasure to see the damage you've done?'

He swung to face her.

'Why behave like this?' she raved, unable to stop. 'What difference does it make to you whether there's a holiday village here or not? It could bring life to the area. Jobs. Money.'

'Yes!' he snarled. 'That would have to come into it sooner or later. After all——' his voice dripped sarcasm '—that's your yardstick for every damned thing in this world, isn't it?'

Struck by the venom in his voice, she quickly recovered. 'What are you talking about? Of course money comes into it! It costs millions to build a place like this. It costs money to make a dream come true!'

Somehow they were standing within inches of each other again. He grasped her arm as she swivelled away, unable to bear such nearness. He yanked her round to face him. 'It costs, Shelley! Yes! And not just money,' he rasped into her face. His fingers bit into her arm. 'I learned what it costs to dream during one long, hot, never-to-be-forgotten summer. Well, now I have the millions. And I can have what I want.'

'What do you want?' she demanded, flushing with the effect his touch had on her.

'You can guess, surely?' The corners of his lips indented. 'I want you.'

She looked at him in stupefaction. 'What did you say?'

'I want you,' he repeated. 'You're going to be my bride.'

'Bride?' she echoed, voice rising in disbelief. When he didn't deny it she said hoarsely, 'Are you mad? After what you've done? I hate you!' A hysterical laugh escaped before she could stop it. 'You must think I'm some kind of naïve idiot.'

He was looking murderously down at her, black eyes flashing with unnerving danger.

'I wouldn't marry you if you were the last man on earth!'

'You will,' he replied. 'I've already made up my mind.'

With a gasp she wrested one arm free and tried to bring it up, but he responded so quickly that she hardly knew what had happened. He gripped both her hands behind her in one hand, then lifted the other to tilt her chin. When her lips were adjusted to the correct angle he slid his hand around her waist and enveloped her mouth with his own.

Her defiance lasted for a full second before the betraying surge of desire made her lips open of their own accord beneath the seductive pressure of his.

He released her. 'QED?'

'What does it prove?' she muttered, bringing up her fingertips to her burning mouth. Her head lifted. 'It proves you're still an opportunist. Just like Dad said.'

'My God, nothing changes,' he grated. 'There was no limit to the insults you and your family handed out. I hoped things might have changed. But I was wrong to hope.'

His derisive laugh stung her. 'I will not listen to any more. You will not browbeat me, Christos Kiriakis! Take your hands off me or I shall——'

'Yes?' He quirked one sceptical brow.

Shelley felt a sudden spasm of electricity shoot through her, a mixture of latent desire and fear that she had somehow stepped over some invisible boundary.

They were surrounded by the trappings of civilisation, the things money could provide—the expensive car, the bulldozers and tractors and equipment of her father's commercial enterprise—but what were they against the primitive will of this black-hearted and arrogant male?

He detected the minute change in her response as the realisation struck her, and his voice dropped to a husky snarl. 'You do well to give me that look, my dear Shelley. For once you do not have the upper hand. This is my territory now and I can do anything I want. The truth is, you are still driven by desire, you still want me as much as you did before. And in that respect nothing has changed.'

'Wanted you? I never wanted you!' The outright lie brought a defensive flush to her cheeks, and even though he had not called her lie into question she was compelled to say, 'I was too young to understand what I felt. It wasn't desire. Maybe I was in love with love.'

He laughed outright. 'Wild words, Shelley.'

She became aware that the grip on her arm had altered. It was still firm, but now it became warmer, more sensual. She felt him draw nearer, felt the heat from his aroused body envelop her own and, despite herself, felt her own limbs slacken with the desire for a greater intimacy.

Standing right over her, pressuring her hips against his pelvis, he could see she was breathlessly aware of his arousal. Her body began to ache for him, responding to an ancient pulse, and the desire he spoke of spread in waves until she was unable to prevent her head from tilting in a helpless spasm that must have looked like an invitation.

Not saying anything, and eyes hooded with desire, he brought his lips down to cover her mouth, and against all sense she gave herself to the fever of his kisses, and his voice came to her as if from a distance, ordering her to open her lips. 'Give me your mouth; let me have your lips. Yes, Shelley, give me your mouth as you used to.' And she heard him say it over and over again as he plundered and withdrew and returned again to take more.

When it ended he held her almost reverently, running his mouth over her hair, her neck, lifting his head to examine her flushed face, then letting his lips trail again over her damp forehead and down the pale side of her throat.

'Yes. It shall be,' he murmured at last. 'You cannot say no. You will give me what I want. You will marry me. Come. We've had enough of this place. You've seen all you need to see.'

Trying to grasp some solid fact, she looked over at the building site. It seemed to mirror the confusion in her own mind caused by his astonishing proposal.

She noted the bulldozers lying idly by like stranded prehistoric beasts, the tractors with their toy-box colours, and all the rest of the paraphernalia of such a huge undertaking. They lay in disarray, just as they had been when the contractors had walked off site at the end of their last day's work.

She angled a glance in his direction. 'You knew all along how I would feel to see things like this. You thought it'd make me agree to anything, didn't you?' She pushed a shaky hand through her hair.

Christos was watching her closely. 'If you want a way out, I've told you, you have one.'

She raised her gaze to his.

He turned abruptly and walked over to the Range Rover. She followed, and when she reached him he thrust a slow, measured smile in her direction. 'You understand me, don't you?'

'It's a crazy idea.' Her lips trembled. 'You're saying you'll let work recommence. . .if I marry you? I won't do it!'

His eyes narrowed. 'I must return to the villa.' He climbed into the driver's seat and leaned over to open the passenger door. 'Get in. I have to go back. I have somebody coming over from Paris to meet me —' he glanced at the complicated watch on his wrist '— in about fifteen minutes. I'll drive you to your car. You can come up to the villa to continue this discussion later on.'

He saw her mutinous expression, and his mouth hardened. 'If you don't. . .I'll come and find you.'

She stuck her hands on her hips and glared at him. 'I'll walk back. It isn't far.'

With an impatient scowl he slammed the passenger door, switched on the engine, and over the smooth roar called, 'This is your last chance. Coming?'

'Go to hell!' she shouted.

With a perfunctory wave he slid the car into gear and moved off. Shelley watched him with a mixture of rage and relief.

Surely he couldn't be serious about marriage in exchange for Burton's access to the site? Did he see it as revenge to marry the girl who was once thought to be too good for him? It must be a crazy mix of lust and pride. One thing was clear: stopping work down here was a calculated move in the devious game he had engineered.

Furious at having to walk all the way back up the

hill, she set off, thoughts and feelings intertwined in hopeless confusion.

Where he had touched her seemed to burn like fire. After nine years it had taken just a couple of brief encounters to summon up the old yearning in all its primitive strength.

She recalled those idyllic weeks they had spent together. He had reappeared early the next morning after their calamitous arrival. 'I am Christos. I show you town. Come.' It was the beginning.

They spent every available minute together after that. Her father and Paula, as newly-weds, were too wrapped up in themselves to notice, so long as Shelley wasn't away from the yacht for too long during the day. Every evening she had to have dinner with them at some expensive restaurant or other, but the rest of the time she followed Christos trustingly wherever he led, down hair-raising mountain roads on a borrowed moped, to secret coves, to the ruins of the fortress, or, the bikes parked, strolling hand in hand round the tiny streets of Kassiópi or visiting the lace market in Kérkira.

He first kissed her in the empty garden of his father's taverna one morning before it opened. She remembered how he had drawn away as if afraid he was being too rough for her. After that it had been difficult not to touch, fingers twining, lips brushing, his strong arm round her waist as he showed her his island.

It was safe despite their ardour, for they were rarely alone. There were always people in the streets or down by the quay shouting, '*Yasoo, Christos!*' Everyone knew him. She understood he was teased about his rich foreign girlfriend, though his bleak glance soon cut to size anyone who went too far.

Then came the suggestion to go to the caves at Paleokastritsas. Christos turned up in his speedy little outboard early that morning and they set off for a day of swimming and sightseeing at what was one of the main tourist attractions. It was a magical day, but disaster struck when they tried to set off back. The engine was completely dead.

Muttering Greek curses, Christos took it apart, spreading the pieces out on the rocks, then put it expertly back together, but it still refused to work. By this time all the other tourists had gone, the tide was coming in and there was nothing for it but to wait until the ebb, climb the cliff, and find shelter until it was light enough to risk setting off across country. Even so, it had been a treacherous walk across the boulder-strewn hillside in the half-light of that summer's morning.

It was still early next morning when Shelley, dishevelled and weary, climbed back on board *Aphrodite*.

Paula, looking pale without her make-up, was lying in wait.

'Thank goodness you're safe!' Her spontaneous relief turned to anger at once. 'But where have you been? We've been up all night worrying about you. Your father had to call the police, but all they said was to wait till morning. He's half out of his mind. Get down to see him at once.'

Christos tried to come on board. 'I tell your father, Shelley. My blame.'

Paula barred his way. 'Don't dare set foot on this

yacht, you barbarian! And keep away from this child. She is not for you!' Then she hustled her shocked stepdaughter down the companionway. 'How could you do this to us?' she hissed in her ear.

Full of apologies, Shelley tried to explain what had happened.

'Engine failure? It's the oldest trick in the book!' derided Paula. 'Anyway, it's what happened after the engine failed we're worried about.'

'Nothing happened,' Shelley protested. Her father, grim-faced, saw her come into the cabin with obvious relief, then demanded to know what had happened. She told her story on a rising note of hysteria when it was clear he wasn't going to believe a word.

'It was an accident,' she repeated. 'Christos did his best to repair the engine. But it was no good. After sheltering in some ruins we set off to walk back as soon as it was light enough.' He was giving her a hard look. 'We had to walk for ages. Eventually we met a farmer in a mule cart and he gave us a lift to the edge of town.'

Nothing prepared her for her father's rage. 'I want the truth!' Colin Burton thundered. 'I won't punish you, but I must know how far it went!'

At first she didn't grasp his fears. When she blindly repeated the same story there was disbelief on his face. Then came that humiliating scene when, trailed by a now weeping Paula, he accosted old Mr Kiriakis in his taverna.

Oblivious to the speculative glances of the customers, he raged into the busy kitchens and demanded to know where Christos was. Mr Kiriakis took a minute to understand what was going on, then he defended his son in a torrent of furious Greek.

Brought on the scene by all the shouting, Christos appeared from an upstairs room, but instead of coming to Shelley's side, as she hoped and prayed, he took his father by the arm and spoke to him in a rapid, unhappy voice.

Further tirades ensued between the two older men, neither really understanding the other. Shelley, the focus of all eyes, prayed that Christos would deny sleeping with her, but he didn't. He simply glared, stone-faced, his expression unchanging, as if willing her to deny she had ever had anything to do with him.

But she felt too shell-shocked to say anything. After one searing look from those black eyes she could barely meet his glance again. Shame blurred her eyes and she had to bite her lower lip to keep from crying. Why couldn't he tell them that nothing had happened? Too shocked to defend herself, she could only stare at the ground until she felt Paula grasp her by the arm and pull her away.

The shouting continued out in the street as Mr Kiriakis all but threw them out of his taverna. Worse was to hear him suggest in his halting English that Greek boys despised foreign girls for being so available. Their own Corfiot girls were so strictly brought up that they never went out alone with a boy until they were going to marry him.

She felt she could have died of shame. Crying herself to sleep that night, she thought it must be because he secretly despised her that Christos had kept silent.

What she saw as betrayal became a turning-point in her life. She had never been so trusting since.

When she reached the car she climbed unhappily inside. The tracks of the Range Rover led her back up the dusty trail, past the old Greek guarding the barrier, and on to the road. Soon she was back in the busy town. It seemed amazing to find the market still in full swing. She felt she'd been to the ends of the earth and back since driving out that morning.

Arriving at the house, she found Anna about to serve lunch. 'Had a nice drive, Shelley?' she asked. 'Is good timing. Now we eat!'

All the rest of that day she expected some word from Christos. Mentally she braced herself for the encounter. But there was nothing.

To Spyro she said, 'We have to take legal advice. In the meantime we must be patient. Once he realises we're going to fight back, he'll come to his senses.'

She couldn't tell him about the offer Christos had made.

Spyro looked across at his wife as she sat making lace in the window. The children were in bed and the house was washed by a deep domestic calm. 'You remember Kiriakis, my Anna?'

Her placid features broke into a soft smile. 'Ah, Christos,' she murmured.

Spyro reached out to touch her knee. 'What's this, Anna?' He looked put out.

She placed one hand over his and squeezed in gentle reassurance. 'We crazy girls.' She smiled. 'How we watched from behind the shutters this young lion!'

Spyro planted a possessive kiss on her cheek.

Later in her room Shelley wondered how she could sound so efficient when her mind was torn into little bits with scraps of memory jostling with the facts.

Anna's comment had aroused a host of unwilling memories, and she couldn't help but compare the Christos of today with the tanned twenty-year-old she had been mad about.

Even then there had been that latent force, the impatience, the sense of power, and in a strange way a sense of authority; witness the way he had taken charge of things when *Aphrodite*'s propeller shaft had snagged.

But the years had added something to him. When as a younger man he had been energetic and full of an insatiable vitality, with a reckless drive that sometimes led him into trouble, it was now contained, all the more impressive because it had substance. It was a more potent force because it was consciously directed.

It was as if he had some hunger inside him, she thought, a hunger that had to be satisfied at any price.

She turned restlessly in the small bed. In the warm stillness of the night, no matter how hard she tried, she simply couldn't get him out of her thoughts.

Today the memory of the primeval shock she had felt on first meeting him had forced itself from out of her subsconscious, where it had safely lain. What would it be like to become his bride? It was madness even to contemplate it.

Even Anna, placid wife and mother, had recognised the danger of a man like Christos. A 'lion', she had called him.

CHAPTER FIVE

Two days had gone by. Still no word. Shelley restlessly sunbathed on her balcony. He was winding her nerves like watch springs.

She got up yet again when she heard the phone. But Anna's voice came in a chatter of Greek.

Shelley went back and slapped some more suntan oil on her arms and legs. She had got into the Greek way of life without any trouble, coffee with Anna, chatting to Spyro, enjoying long, leisurely meals in the garden. But it was all on the surface. Inside she was as nervy as a kitten. She looked over the balcony.

The children were playing down there. When they saw her they shouted for her to come and play. They were all firm friends by now. She waved back.

First she had better ring Malcolm.

'Still no news from Kiriakis,' she told him when she got through.

'Stay put,' he told her yet again.

'I'm just so worried about Dad,' she confessed.

'He's still convalescent. I'm going to keep the news from him for as long as I can, so as not to worry him unduly.'

She warned him that the Greek Orthodox Easter was coming up. 'There'll be no chance of doing any business for four or five days. But after that it's going to be a worry, keeping the contractors on stand-by.'

'Spyro will have that side under control,' he reminded her. 'Don't worry, Shelley. As soon as you can meet this Kiriakis fellow again and put our case, he'll see reason. I have every faith in you,' he added. 'We all have.'

That only seemed to make things worse. 'I don't think you understand what he's like,' she warned.

'You can handle him, Shelley. But,' he added, 'whatever you do, don't come back here yet. We have far more control over the situation if one of us is on the spot.'

'I wasn't thinking of coming back, much as I long to,' she added with feeling. 'But I can't help thinking you're underestimating him.'

'Don't fail. We're counting on you.'

Stifling the nervous qualms this last remark aroused, she told him Spyro and Anna had insisted she stay on with them. 'But they can't have expected me to stay with them as long as this.'

'The Corfiots are very hospitable people,' he told her. 'I'm glad I know where to find you.'

At this echo of Christos's words her thoughts plunged back to him.

On an impulse she rang his office. An assistant told her Mr Kiriakis was out of the country.

That at least told her why he hadn't summoned her to the villa.

Just then she heard the rush of feet as all four children ran into the house. They scampered along the tiled passage to one of the rooms at the front of the house. There were some stifled giggles, then a deathly hush.

It was broken by the most ear-shattering sound from outside. It was like a hundred dinner-services being smashed wholesale on to the cobbled street.

Shelley rushed into the room, alarm turning to astonishment when she saw them all heaving plates out of the window. She would have stopped them at once if Anna and Spyro hadn't been standing unperturbed beside them.

Anna turned. 'Here, Shelley, you too!' She pushed three or four plates into Shelley's startled grasp.

The heavy plates nearly slipped from her fingers. They were certainly not the best china!

Spyro came over. 'No, don't drop them in here! Throw them out of the window! Look, like this!'

Obviously itching to copy the children, he heaved a plate through the opening, sending it in a skimming arc to land with a smash in the middle of the street.

Young Niko tried to copy his father, but his aim was wild and the plate landed on the pavement. Undeterred, he had another go, Spyro proudly encouraging him with a few fatherly tips on how to improve.

Even little Theodora had to have a try, being lifted up to the windowsill in her mother's arms to let the big plate slide from between her tiny fingers. Everyone applauded when it hit the ground and splintered into a few pieces. She giggled shyly and hid her face in her mother's hair.

Amused by Shelley's dumbfounded expression, Anna explained, 'We are throwing out the devil, don't you see? Is old custom. It lets go of anger, helps good sleep at night!'

Shelley fingered the plates Spyro had given her. 'I'd better have a go.' She took aim. There was one devil she wanted to throw out! Unable to hold back a grimace, she hurled a couple of plates into the street. She saw them whiz violently through the air and come to land with a resounding smash on the other side. One for Christos! she thought. And another! as a second one followed it.

'This is really satisfying,' she said feelingly as her fingers closed over plate after plate.

She was giggling along with everybody else by the time they came to the end of the pile. They had been specially manufactured for the occasion, and the street was covered in broken plates where the neighbours had been doing the same thing.

'I haven't enjoyed myself so much for ages!' she exclaimed. If only she could throw off the effects of Christos's domination so easily!

Everybody was in a good mood afterwards, even the men who came round with big brooms to sweep away all the shards of broken crockery, and the sense of exhilaration lasted the rest of the day. After supper Spyro invited her to join him and a group of friends.

'Tonight we follow the *epitaphios* with our lighted candles,' he told her. 'What is this word in English?'

Shelley rummaged around in her shoulder-bag for her phrase book. 'It says "pall" here. Is that right?' She looked puzzled.

Spyro nodded. 'Sure. That's just what it is. The funeral pall of Saint Spyridon, the patron saint of

Corfu. We take his effigy out of the church and carry it about to let him have a look round his town to make sure everything is OK!' He laughed.

'Is very pretty, Shelley,' said Anna. 'Decorated with a thousand candles. It is the Good Friday procession after midnight service.'

'You come with us,' invited Spyro. 'Taste Corfiot life to the full!'

Anna stayed behind with the children, but quite a crowd of people from the same street made their way to the big church on the square.

Dressed in their best, they climbed the steps to seats in a balcony that ran right round between the decorated pillars and gave a good view into the crowded nave below.

It seemed to Shelley that almost the whole community had squashed into the magnificent old building. Much against her will she found herself helplessly combing the crowd for one particular face among the many, wondering if he was back already from his business trip. There were plenty of black-haired men, features gilded by candlelight in the Byzantine shadows, but none was the one she sought.

When the long service began she tried as best she could to follow the complicated ritual led by the priests in their gold and purple robes. But soon she began to feel sleepy. In fact she was sure she nodded off once or twice, jerking guiltily upright as she felt her head drop, dreams and reality fusing in a blur of black and gold under the heady perfume of burning incense.

The third time her head drooped she tried to make a more determined effort to stay awake, fixing her eyes firmly on the sea of faces opposite. Then she really did wake up, leaning forward with a sharp gasp. Something about one of the profiles among the people facing them sent a jolt of recognition through her.

The man turned to stare down into the nave, and Shelley hardly dared to breathe while she waited for him to turn to face her again. But before he did the lights began to go out, and in a moment darkness dropped like a veil between the balconies.

After that a single voice began to resonate above the chanting of the crowd, echoing and re-echoing through the inky darkness of the church in convoluted ascents and descents as it reached towards the climax of the service. Its exotic half-tones and broken rhythms suggested an ancient music both spiritual and sensual, and infinitely erotic in its primitive power.

At a pre-ordained moment silence fell, and after a long pause a tiny light pricked the darkness.

It lit up first the glittering silver of the saint's shrine, picking out the stern, strong features of the gilded effigy, and then another candle was ignited from the first, glittering along the life-like wooden figure in its robes of real silk, and then another and another came alight, revealing yet more of the medieval saint on his catafalque.

Gradually the whole nave began to glow with candlelight, a carpet of flame swaying in the hands of the congregation as they began to follow the effigy. From above it looked like a shining river, a lava flow of light moving with stately pace between the stone pillars.

Shelley watched the people opposite begin to light their own candles from those of their neighbours, and again she found herself looking for that profile she had glimpsed before the lights went out, fearing and longing for it at the same time.

But if it had been Christos, he had gone.

Relief and disappointment flooded through her.

Below them the great carved doors were flung open to allow the river of light into the street, and, following Spyro and his friends, she carried the slender white taper he had given her, one hand shielding the guttering flame from draughts. The crowd carried her with it in a slow procession in the wake of the silver *epitaphios*, awash with candlelight.

It was a heady experience and aroused a strange and unexplainable mood. She had never been part of celebrations like this before, and although she couldn't understand the chanting of the crowd she felt a primitive bond with her surroundings, especially when the procession moved across the road to the beach and out along the sands to the very edge of the softly surging tide. Overhead the purple sky scattered its own candlelight, as if to mirror that below.

Suddenly her dream-thoughts were interrupted by a touch on the arm. Strong fingers grasped her, dragging her from the crowd.

'Going native, dear Shelley?' rasped a familiar voice.

She peered into the darkness, then raised the

candle as if to confirm what she already knew. 'I knew I'd seen you in the church,' she whispered.

His voice was harsh. 'With your blonde hair floating round your shoulders you look like one of St Spyridon's angels. Especially with this elegant stage prop shedding its glow over your face.'

Out of the darkness a finger reached into the circle of light and began to travel along the stem of white wax until it reached her own hand, where it stopped. She felt him cup it, transmitting a thrill of instant warmth to her skin.

'Why are you here, Christos?'

His lips drew back. 'I would have thought that was obvious.' He brought his black brows together. 'I'm here to have your answer.'

'What answer?' Her mouth turned stubborn, dreading his response.

He closed his almond eyes with impatience. 'Don't play games. I want your response to my offer of marriage.'

'Offer? I thought it was an ultimatum.'

'We can be civilised about this.'

'How, when you offer no alternative?'

'There is an alternative. Obviously.'

'What alternative? To allow you to destroy my father's dreams and with them probably his health and his life too?'

'It is your choice.' His mouth was hard.

Tears of frustration and anger sprang to her eyes. 'You know it won't work. Marriage is supposed to mean something to the participants.'

His brow darkened. The leaping light from the candle revealed every nuance of his black mood.

'Let me put it clearly and finally.' His tone was harsh. 'You want to save your father's dream project. I have offered a way out. It's simple. Marry me, and there will be no opposition. Decline, and. . .' He give a dismissive shrug of the broad shoulders beneath the black jacket. 'Why should I make concessions to strangers, to business rivals, to those not of my family? It's a simple proposition.'

'It should be a proposal, not a proposition,' she jerked out.

'My English is not so good, no?'

'It's good enough and you damn well know it.' Her glance flew wildly round the chanting crowd, but there was no help there, and it dragged reluctantly back to his brooding features. He watched in silence as an inner struggle took place, and at last she whispered, 'You give me no real choice.'

He gave a growl of satisfaction. 'Say it,' he commanded. 'I want to hear the word on your lips.'

The white wax taper shook in her hand, sending shadows leaping across the gaunt hollows of his face as he stared down at her.

Wishing him in hell, she whispered, 'Yes.' Then she couldn't bear it any longer. 'Yes,' she shouted above the crowd. 'You know I have to. Yes! Yes! Now leave me alone!' With a sob she turned to get away, but, smiling with grim satisfaction, he lowered his head to put his lips close to her ear.

'Be ready at ten tomorrow morning. We have much to discuss. A car will pick you up from the house.'

Before she could utter a word of protest he had melted into the darkness and the chanting crowd swayed round her, languidly blocking her attempts to go after him.

Just then Spyro appeared beside her. 'I though I'd lost you, Shelley. Come, we go home now.'

Her candle was still alight when they finally reached the house. Anna was sitting up, the baby asleep in her arms. She observed the flame with approval. 'This mean good luck for the year ahead,' she told her.

Shelley couldn't repress a hollow laugh as she contemplated the nature of her luck at present.

Next morning she felt like smashing plates again. What had she done? It was like a nightmare. There was no way out. Christos, she knew, would never let her go now she had given her word. Her thoughts flew to ways of escape, but the repercussions would be even worse now, and heaven knew what sort of revenge he might be tempted to exact at a deliberately broken promise.

She tried to go about her normal routine, but she couldn't stop shaking. Twice she changed her clothes before she felt she was ready, and she stood for an age on the balcony with a hairbrush in her hand, not knowing what to do.

Fool, she told herself as she went back inside to do her hair. As she raked the brush through it she realised it still smelt of incense. It made the presence of Christos in the room almost real.

Pull yourself together, she warned. The beach project had to be saved. It could mean the difference between life or death for her father.

Too distracted to wash her hair, she left it as it

was, dug out a plain black dress from her wardrobe, and changed for the third time. The way she felt now, like a sacrifice to some malevolent demon, black was a suitable colour. It was high-necked and sleeveless, falling to just above the knee, and it made her feel strong and in control, even if she wasn't.

Despite her rage against Christos, she yearned for some sign that he cared for her. But human feeling seemed to be the last quality he possessed.

Slipping her bare feet into a pair of high-heeled sandals, she was downstairs by the time the hall clock struck ten.

Almost to the minute there was a brisk rap on the door. Calling out to Anna in the kitchen, she braced herself as she went to open it. It was Christos's uniformed chauffeur.

'*Kalimera.*' He nodded.

She called back over her shoulder, 'I'm just off, Anna. Expect me when you see me! *Adio!*' Then she followed him to the car.

After a silent drive in the Rolls to the Villa Monasco they swept up the drive just as a helicopter was taking off from a landing-pad at the side of the building. Immediately Christos himself came sprinting down the steps, wearing jeans and a dark blue, open-necked shirt. He climbed abruptly into the car with instructions to the driver that Shelley was unable to follow.

His glance raked her pale features, but she was in too much turmoil to demand to know where he was taking her. They sat in silence, but, luckily, before it

could bring her shattered nerves to breaking-pitch
the car came to a halt. They left the driver spreading
his morning paper over the dashboard to wait, and,
with Christos taking the lead, they walked along a
natural promontory towards the cliffs. Shelley tried
to pretend there was nothing more important on her
mind than sightseeing.

It was a beautiful stretch of countryside, and if he
wanted to remind her how magnificent his island was
he was succeeding. Hills spread in ever deepening
shades of cobalt and lavender to the dim distance,
while beneath their feet across the south-facing
headland they trod on a carpet of a myriad spring
flowers. Foams of blossom swept the meadows far
below, and she lost count of the different kind of
flowers near at hand. It was a collector's paradise,
she realised, every colour under the sun represented
in some miniature form or other. In any other
circumstances it would have been heaven.

There was a ruin at the end of the path, and
something about it struck her as familiar. As they
came closer she realised it was the real thing, a
genuine Greek temple. The purity of its white columns was enhanced by the amethyst of sea and sky
behind it.

'Remember this?' Something in the tone of his
voice made her give him a sharp glance, but his
expression was as enigmatic as ever.

'How could I remember?' She looked down at the
double row of white columns. Then her face
blanched. The last time she had seen the temple was
one summer's morning at dawn, nine years ago.

When she had given herself time to recover she swung back to face him.

'You don't remember?' He was examining every nuance of her features.

'Why should I?' She dropped her glance.

He jerked away and gazed down the slope towards the ruin. 'It is dedicated to the goddess Aphaia,' he said at last.

She gave him a swift sideways glance. Why was he doing this? Why try to evoke memories of the past? He must know how much anguish it caused to remember that time. Unwanted, memory came scudding back. Christos had tried to tell her about Aphaia, his rich voice making the single word sound like a magic incantation. Then had followed some lines in Greek, sounding like poetry. His voice had made her tremble with its sensuality. She could have listened all night.

Later she had looked up the name in the school library to find that Aphaia was a goddess of the moon. She had whispered the name for luck as she fell asleep at night. Despite what had happened, she hadn't been able to help longing for him with every fibre of her being. Just to say the name had made him seem close in those first nightmare days back in England.

Avoiding his glance, she picked her way between the fallen stones and finished up at the bottom of a shallow slope at the entrance. Her mind was teeming, but uppermost was the desire to know why he had decided to bring her here.

When she turned he was leaning against one of the fluted columns. Its slender elegance contrasted with his purely masculine bulk. He could have been carved from stone himself, a perfect example of the ideal male physique.

She stumbled towards him over the loose white stones. His black eyes washed over her upturned face as she approached.

'Down there must be the rocks where we got cut off.' She flushed at the memory.

After climbing up from the caves where they had abandoned the boat when the tide fell, they had sheltered in the temple until it was light enough to risk setting off across country, with its ravines and hidden valleys. Trustingly she had followed wherever he led in the magical half-light of that summer's dawn.

She looked out to sea. From up here the currents were visible like the sinews of a fabled animal at sleep. For a moment she forgot their quarrel. 'This place is so beautiful,' she breathed.

'So are you,' he murmured just behind her.

She turned, drinking in the sight of him, his thick dark hair blown by the breeze across his forehead. 'Am I?' she asked, her voice husky and warmer than she intended.

In reply he gave a hard laugh, his black eyes devoid of expression. 'You know you are. But you will be even more so on our wedding-day.'

When she flinched he said, 'We must make an announcement.' His voice thickened. 'I do not intend to wait long.'

The repressed desire in his voice aroused her own, and she had to fight the impulse to reach out to him, to touch him, to run her fingers through his strong dark hair. It was so strong that it threatened to swamp her outrage at what he was forcing her to do.

Trembling with the force of the conflict, she was amazed at herself for wanting to respond to what was nothing more than an animal excitement in his voice.

She jerked round, staring blindly out to sea, pretending to admire the view. In reality she was conscious of nothing but the penetration of his black glance.

'Shelley!' came his urgent tones. 'Turn back and look at me.'

'I have done.' Her voice was out of control.

'I said turn to me.' Despite her intention, she longed to witness the expression that could accompany such a husky sensuality. She found herself turning a degree in his direction, before yielding completely, swivelling to throw at him a defiant glare.

'Yes.' His voice was husky too. 'I know you must remember.'

His caressing tone conjured up the past, as it was meant to. Against her will it swam sharply into focus. That night. That endless night. She remembered the stars crowding the sky. The new moon. His protective arms. The sudden flare of bewildering desire that had made her trail her fingers through his thick black hair.

But he had quenched her explorations with a savage gesture, saying in his beautiful broken English, 'Shelley, I want to love you. But I must not. I am your protector. Is all I am for now.'

She gave him a sharp glance. Was this what he wanted her to remember?

Despite his warning, her arms had reached out for him, fingers running helplessly and innocently through the shining strands, longing to discover the unfamiliar male shape. . . It had been on this hillside amid the scent of wild thyme, her natural shyness pierced by her adoration.

But his chivalry had been impregnable. It had only been by dint of his supreme control that things had not gone further. She blushed even now to remember how he had been the one to call things to a halt.

Was it this he wished her to remember?

Her thoughts were bitter. It was that younger Christos, full of pride and conscious of his honour, who had won her heart and, only a short while later, to her horror and disbelief, discarded it.

Afraid he could see into her mind, she moved away. His brooding gaze pursued her. Ignoring it, she picked her way to the far side of the ruin, as if trying to get a closer look at the place where they had had to scramble to safety. Her cheeks were burning.

He followed, coming up behind her and leaning near to ask in a resonant growl, 'See it? We were trapped there many hours, with the moon sliding over the heavens. I watched over you, saw you sleep, saw you dream, saw you slowly wake as Aphaia slid into the sea.'

She half turned, but couldn't read his thoughts, even though he was standing so close. She tingled when his hard body brushed her.

'Your hair smells of incense, Shelley,' she heard him say.

Before she could prevent it he reached out to lift one of her escaping tendrils, allowing the silvery strand to trail through his fingers, at the last minute bringing it to his face to inhale the heady perfume with an expression of raw sensuality.

The gesture took her senses by storm. Already she was beginning to waver. It felt like melting, she thought, bones turning soft, muscles becoming as molten as honey. There was a powerful inevitability when he took her into his arms. She found she could focus on nothing but his lips as they hovered above her own mouth. Her breasts seemed to grow full, pressing against the thin black cotton of her dress to yearn towards him. A pool of heat between her thighs seemed to spread, engulfing her entire frame in its fires.

'Christos,' she whispered, feverish with doubt. His motives were still unclear. Yet, unable to stop herself, she tasted his name on her lips, blue eyes devouring his dark features.

One hand came up, either to draw him close or to fend him off. She fingered the cool silk of his shirt in a gesture of indecision. On the brink of something extraordinary, she still shrank back from the small move that would betray the depths of her emotions.

The heady knowledge of what it was like to be kissed by him inched her towards surrender. This time there would be no surprise, only a sort of exquisite fatefulness.

But Christos himself delayed the moment, bringing up one of his own hands and sheltering her fingers in it. His voice was hoarse. 'Such a priceless prize. No wonder your father defended your honour with such vigour nine years ago.'

He gave a sudden harsh, disowning laugh, jarring her romantic dream, the momentary softness in his expression once again turning hard and impenetrable. But then she saw her own longing mirrored in his eyes. As if he didn't wish it, his mouth came down over hers.

He kissed her exploratively at first. Then something inside her released itself and she found herself responding with a thirsty longing, as if nothing would satisfy her but to drain him and to be drained by him to the last drop of resistance.

But just as suddenly as he had unreined his desire he released her, stepping back, severing contact, eyes momentarily closing as if with the strain of fighting to master his obvious desire.

She found herself searching his face for some sign to allay the doubts shooting like poisoned darts into her mind, but his face was like a mask as he looked back at her. He seemed to weigh the effect of his kiss without any sign of emotion.

Embarrassment at how ardently she had responded, betraying her inmost feelings to a man who appeared only interested in using her for his own mysterious ends, spasmed through her.

His voice came hard and cold. 'Yes, your father will surely regret leaving you to this man Fitch. The poor fool handed you to me like a gift. If I were your father I would make sure it cost him his job.'

She felt as if she had been dealt a physical blow.

What was he saying? How could he be so full of desire one moment and so callous the next?

Something cold seemed to flow over her skin. But he drew his lips back in a semblance of a smile, though his eyes were as enigmatic as ever as he brought her possessively back into his arms.

The air was electric between them.

'Don't you understand anything, Shelley? Has nothing I have said revealed anything about me?' His voice vibrated.

'You've revealed how obstinate you are, and. . .' She ducked her head, not wishing to engage in all the old arguments.

He prompted, 'And?'

'And I find you c-confusing,' she managed. Her glance was compelled to linger over the fastidious features angled down at her. Shivering, she was aware of his body heat, the desire engulfing them both. She shook her head. 'Nothing you do makes sense,' she defended on a small breath.

He gazed out towards the blue Ionian, as if seeking inspiration from its sparkling waves.

'I am guilty of a little machinating. Is that the word?' Before she could reply he went on, 'I have been watching your father's holiday village for some time. I knew he bought up land nine years ago. I myself have had a project or two going here over the years, and my friends on the island have always kept me informed. I bought up the land leading to the peninsula six months ago. It struck me it would give me a very strong position.'

'For what?' she managed. She was puzzled.

'Knowing you were trouble-shooter for your

father's European operations, it was obvious that in
the event of any trouble out here you would be sent
to fix it.' He gave a satisfied smile. 'I knew Fitch was
in charge of your London office and your father was
in St Lucia, recuperating.'

'You conniving devil!' she exploded.

'Yes, that's true,' he agreed. 'But it was the only
way. I had decided I would get you out here. Then I
would marry you.'

'But why, in heaven's name?' It was obvious the
little matter of love had never entered his head.
Desire, yes. But for a man like Christos desire
plainly didn't imply marriage. 'Why?' she demanded
more quietly when he didn't reply at once.

His voice roughened. 'It suits my purposes. That
is all you need to know.'

His black eyes probed her expression. 'It is fitting
that I have you,' he told her, voice like ice.

She lifted pained eyes to his. Had he really
planned it in such cold, calculating detail?

It was like a strange dream where what she had
once desired was now hers for the taking. Yet the
gift was a poisoned chalice because it didn't come
with love. He hadn't mentioned the word. For him
it seemed to be an irrelevance. He uncoiled from
beside her, immediately businesslike.

'Later you shall have a tour of your new home.
But first we have things to do, then lunch and a
social engagement.'

Having coolly informed her of their programme
for the rest of the day, he began to turn away as if
expecting her to follow. Then he pivoted, his brooding eyes strangely reticent. 'Believe it or not, I didn't

intend to rush you. But having brought you out here, why waste time with preliminaries? Besides, I am sure you would have seen through the wine and roses in a flash.'

He turned again and began to stride briskly towards the car.

CHAPTER SIX

As THE car set off Shelley tried to organise her thoughts. Why should Christos go to such lengths to lure her to Corfu to marry her? In the old days Paula's accusation that he was a penniless fortune-hunter might have had a superficial plausibility. But not now. He was impressively wealthy in his own right.

Eventually she was driven back to the idea that it was all a kind of personal vendetta. The more she thought about it, the more unlikely it seemed that it was anything else.

It was because of what had happened nine years ago. Because of that very public insult meted out by her father. Now he was out for revenge. And she was his sacrificial victim.

She turned to him, ready to blurt her suspicions, but before a single word could spring to her lips he placed one index finger over the soft bow. Black eyes fixed intently on her mouth, he slowly shook his head.

The moment seemed to drag, while the pressure of his touch fluttered her nerves with alarm. She was conscious of a violent desire for the moment to lengthen into infinity. But eventually he slid his finger away with a smouldering glance at her flushed cheeks. Her lips parted at the loss, tongue flicking over the place where she could feel the ghost of his caress.

'I shall have no buts from you, Shelley,' he murmured. 'You have given your word. There is no going back.'

He touched his fingertip to her lips again, the intimacy of the gesture at odds with the coldness of his words, and, despite the presence of the chauffeur, concentrating firmly on his driving, his mouth began to lower to the lips imprisoned beneath his splayed fingers.

She felt his own lips tease hers, touching, pressuring, until he seemed convinced he had subdued her objections. His kiss became a final sealing of the pact between them.

She felt the full pressure of his mouth on hers with a gasp of spontaneous excitement. His fingers slid in a seductive trail down the length of her throat as he bent over her. He seemed determined to drive home the importance of her promise. Her own lips parted in tacit acceptance.

Pressing her back until she was reclining against the leather seat, his kiss deepened. She forgot everything until he lifted his head and growled, 'When you kiss me like that, I know you say yes to everything.'

His lips hovered just above her own as his eyes held hers with a derisive smile. Just then the car reached the summit of a hill and his gaze jerked to the window. 'Look, we are passing the villa. This is the best view.'

He indicated the white building at the far end of a narrow valley. It looked like a palace, set amid its gardens, with the slash of turquoise between the arches where the corner of a large pool was visible.

He drew her attention to nearby vineyards and to some groves of olive further off. In the distance Mount Pandokrator reared its purple sides.

Still holding her intimately in his arms, he switched without any difficulty to practical talk.

He told her, 'Do you see the land as far as the mountain slope? That is all mine. I also have extensive interests in commercial shipping with a base in Piraeus. As my wife, you will have anything your heart desires. Your father will have no cause for objection when you tell him.'

His eyes burned into her own, holding them with an obvious challenge.

She managed to drag her glance from his, staring mutely out of the window at this evidence of his financial power. It brought her no joy to know she would be the wife of such a wealthy man. What did it matter when she meant nothing more to him than a symbol of his triumph?

She bit her lip hard, fighting back hot tears of anguish, then forced herself to meet his gaze.

Reluctantly she gave a remote smile. 'It's very impressive.' She gave a cursory glance back over the scene before adding, 'But you surely don't expect me to be dancing for joy, do you, knowing that I'm being forced into a marriage against my will?'

He gave a frown. 'You will get used to the idea if you make a little effort.' He tilted her chin up and looked long and intently into her eyes. 'I am happy. Very happy.' His voice was a murmur as soft as a caress.

She lowered her lids to avoid a look that seemed about to devour her, feeling he was able to read her mind in the swimming of her eyes, from what he saw there, aware of the humiliating fact that she was floundering on the brink of total surrender whenever he touched her. She had lowered her lids to veil the truth from his probing glance. Never would she admit how he moved her.

When his lips brushed her own it came as a small shock, but the moment was over in an instant. When she opened her eyes they were pulling to a halt outside a wrought-iron gate set in a high white wall. Through the iron bars she had an impression of rampant greenery.

They got out and Christos led Shelley through the gate. They were in a walled garden, the whole place a riot of lush growth trimmed into artless patterns of shape and texture. The thick, almost animal stumps of old cactus plants rose to the level of the upper window of a house, and the spiny shapes of sub-tropical grasses, sharp fronds of aloha and shiny wax-like palms grew in profusion on both sides of a narrow path.

Christos had to stoop in order to lead the way through a tunnel of climbing roses. It led directly to the white front door of a pretty stone-built house.

It was a building of modest size, Shelley noticed, but incredibly picturesque, like a doll's house, with white shutters and pots of bright flowers along the wall, and everything in spotless condition.

Unable to restrain her curiosity, she asked, 'Whose house is it?'

Christos had already reached the front door. He

swivelled on the well scrubbed step. 'She doesn't speak a word of English.' He paused. 'Don't let that worry you.'

'But whose house is it?' she asked again, somehow already suspecting the answer.

'You have to meet my mother. She will want to know we intend to set a date.'

Shelley blanched. But he had already pressed open the door, and she pushed blindly into the dark entrance after him. Hesitating, she found herself in a stone-flagged hall. It was scattered with one or two traditional wool rugs, and the air was scented by the lavender massed in stone pots.

Calling out something in his own language, Christos strode on into one of the rooms, and she heard him greet someone inside. She lagged behind, shy at the prospect of meeting his mother, frightened at the thought that they were to set an actual date for the wedding. It made the whole nightmare hideously real.

Realising she couldn't hide outside forever, she stepped over the threshold.

Christos was murmuring something in Greek to a slight figure in black lying on a basketwork sofa piled with lacy cushions. When Shelley appeared he straightened, holding out one hand to present her.

She was conscious of bright eyes watching her from the lined face of a woman in her sixties, her high cheekbones made more prominent by a severe chignon of greying hair. Evidently she had been ill, for she was lying with her feet up, shoulders wrapped in a black lace shawl. Her faded beauty was accented by the velvet ribbon pinned at her throat by a gold cameo brooch.

When her glance met Shelley's she held out both hands. Shelley moved forward, reaching out to take the delicate fingers in her own. Mrs Kiriakis murmured something, but Shelley couldn't even begin to understand.

She turned to Christos for help. His glance was fixed intently on her face. 'She is saying, "Welcome to the house of Kiriakis".'

Shelley felt the importance of the occasion for Christos's mother. She bent her head to her, wondering if she suspected the true nature of her son. At this moment Christos was as compliant as a well tamed tabby. His swift change to this smiling, urbane manner sent her mind reeling.

Pulling herself together, she asked, '*Tee kanees*?'—how are you? She felt a fool trying out her halting Greek in front of Christos when he was so fluent in several languages himself. When she looked up she dared him to laugh, but to her astonishment he gave her an encouraging smile.

Christos brought forward one of the cushioned chairs for her to sit on. His black glance washed impassively over her face as he came to sit on the edge of her chair. It creaked, taking his weight. She was strongly aware of the hard, muscular male length of him pressing against her. But she couldn't move without making it look obvious she was trying to get away.

While she pretended nothing was amiss, his mother began tugging at one of the many rings she wore. She gave a smiling glance at her son as she fumbled for Shelley's hand.

Before she realised what was happening she discovered that Mrs Kiriakis was pushing an impressive antique ring on to one of her fingers.

'But——' she began when she saw what was happening.

He pressed his mouth to her ear as if they were lovers. 'No buts,' he warned.

The threat in his word belied the lightness of his tone. She understood him perfectly. This was part of the act. 'It's lovely.' She flushed with embarrassment at deceiving his mother into thinking she and Christos were madly in love. Plainly this was what she thought.

She took Christos's hand and Shelley's hand and pressed them both together within her own, smiling gently at them both with tears in her eyes.

When they were released Shelley said in furious English, with a smile fixed to her face so his mother wouldn't be upset by what she was saying, 'I hate you Christos. Does your mother really think we're in love? Nothing could be further from the truth!'

His features expressed no response to her outburst. 'I have told her I shall see the priest later today to fix a date. The sooner the better.'

'And the ring?'

'Don't hand it back. She will be devastated if you do. I'll explain when we get outside. Now we must leave.'

Dark eyes tender, he made sure his mother was comfortable, then bent to drop a kiss on her cheek. '*Adio, mama.*'

She gave Shelley a sweet smile and lifted a cheek for a farewell kiss, then lay back among the mound of lacy pillows, lines of fatigue now apparent on her face.

As soon as they were outside Shelley turned to him in fury. 'I feel terrible. Deceit may be second nature to you, but it makes me feel dreadful.'

Christos ignored her comment. 'You got on well. I must say it surprised me.'

There was a moment's pause, then into the silence he informed her, 'You are wearing the ring of the Kiriakises. As my betrothed, you must have it.'

He turned swiftly, and began to head towards the waiting car.

She hurried after him. He stood beside the open door, but she hesitated before climbing in. Lifting the ring, she saw it glitter in the strong sunlight. A twisted gold claw held a cluster of different-coloured stones. It seemed heavy on her finger. She had no right to wear it if it was meant to symbolise love.

As if to confirm her doubts he said, 'It has been worn by Kiriakis brides for two centuries. Many tears of joy and sorrow have been shed over it.'

'So the way I feel now is nothing new?' Her lips trembled. 'Tears of sorrow?' She gave him a cold glance. 'I shall shed no tears over you, Christos. You are forcing this marriage on me when you know it is the last thing I desire.'

His face was white. 'Get into the car.'

'Understand I am agreeing to this charade only to save my father from your vicious schemes.' Head held high, she settled in the opulent rear of the

Rolls. When he climbed in beside her he treated her with frigid politeness, and they drove in silence down the road towards the town.

When they reached the bottom of the hill Christos ordered his driver to proceed through the centre towards a hotel on the esplanade. As they rolled majestically through the seething crowd of shoppers and sightseers, focus of many curious glances, yet insulated within the car, he turned roughly towards her.

'I thought it might have crossed your mind to ask after my father.'

Fury, no doubt due to what she had just said, distorted his normally controlled features.

Shelley opened and closed her mouth. How could she explain why she had failed to mention Mr Kiriakis? Hesitating, she confessed in an almost inaudible voice, 'Last time we met he seemed to hope he would never see me or my family again.'

A memory of the way he had looked her up and down in that awful confrontation at the restaurant came back now with hideous clarity. 'He plainly thought I wasn't worthy of a son of his,' she added. She gave a tight, unhappy smile. 'Where is he?'

Christos gave her a brutal glance. 'He's dead,' he told her.

Her cheeks blanched. 'Dead?'

Christos let his black glance trickle over her face without speaking.

'I'm sorry,' she blurted when the silence lengthened, cobalt eyes swimming. Despite the injustice of what the patriarchal Greek had evidently thought of her, she couldn't prevent a feeling of sorrow wash

over her. His anger had been provoked by Paula's
hysterics and her own father's over-protective rage.

'He died nine years ago.' Christos's voice was taut
and hard.

As she let that fact sink in Christos gave her a
savage glance. 'And do you know how he died?'

Shelley shook her head.

'Let me tell you.' With icy deliberation he forced
her to listen, something cruel in the way he rapped
out the words, accusation in his very tones. Shivers
ran down Shelley's spine as it became clear he saw
the humiliation of that public confrontation as being
instrumental in causing his father's death.

His eyes flashed dangerously. 'In front of that
gawping knot of customers in the restaurant, my
father defended me to the hilt. His pride demanded
it. Even though you gave everyone the impression it
was all true. But after you left he turned on me like
a judge and jury. His trust in me was shattered. He
could scarcely speak for rage at having the Kiriakis
name dragged through the mud. His own son, his
only son, despoiling a virgin, a foreigner, a guest on
our island. What was I made of to behave like that?
Was I an animal?'

'Didn't you insist you were telling the truth?'

'Of course I did. But when you said nothing in my
defence and simply sobbed with that look of complete desolation on your face he didn't believe me.
He was in a rage and said, "I never want you across
my threshold again. You are no son of mine. I
disown you!" By this time I was in a rage myself.
"Can you imagine I would ever set foot in your
house after this?" I told him. "How dare you believe

the word of those people against the word of your
own son? Until the day you admit your mistake I
shall never see you again!" Of course he refused to
back down. So I left.'

His mouth twisted with bitterness and grief. 'That
night, after I had taken a few things and left his
house, the stress proved too much for him. He had
a massive heart attack and died at midnight. I never
received his forgiveness or he mine.'

Deep in confusion, she whispered, 'I'm so sorry,
Christos. I had no idea.' She caught him by the arm,
but her words trailed away when she saw saw his
blistering glance sweep her features.

His lip curled in a chilling smile. 'He died believing the worst of me. If I could have taken you back
as my bride he would have realised he had made a
mistake. He would have had proof that I was a man
of honour. Everyone else would have seen it also as
visible proof of the honour of Christos Kiriakis.'

The suspicion that he only wanted this marriage
to avenge the past was proved conclusively by everything he said.

'You can imagine the scandal in our small town,'
he continued. 'I was branded not only as a seducer
of young girls, but a patricide as well. It caused my
mother much pain.'

'And now, what can she think of me?'

'She has been waiting for you to accept this ring
for many years. Only that one act will redeem the
lost honour of the Kiriakises.'

He gave a hard smile. 'We have no time to lose.
She is frail now after a long illness, and the sooner
the ceremony takes place the better.'

She felt dumb.

'You see, Shelley,' he was continuing, 'you are going to put right the wrong done all those years ago.'

He gave her a long, cold, hard stare. Something changed deep in the black pupils. His face was white, the high cheekbones bruised-looking.

He tapped on the window to tell the driver to stop. They had made desperately slow progress through the buzzing town, but it seemed to Shelley they had travelled a thousand miles. As he prepared to get out she reached out and placed a restraining hand on his arm.

'Christos! Wait!'

Suddenly it was vital that Christos knew her side of the whole tragic mess. 'You don't know my side of the story.'

He fixed her with a penetrating glance. 'Well?'

She found it hard to put into words.

'Dad and Paula didn't let up from the moment I got back on board that morning,' she told him hoarsely. 'They questioned me for ages, convinced I was lying in an attempt to defend you. Dad kept saying, "I know how easy it is to get carried away in the heat of the moment, but you must tell me the truth". He thought you might have made me pregnant,' she admitted bitterly, remembering those anguishing hours.

'And there was Paula, wringing her hands and having hysterics. She seemed to think I'd stayed out deliberately to spoil things between Dad and her. "It's just a way of grabbing attention!" she kept wailing. And then Dad would start in again, "I know you trusted this young ruffian, but you have to accept he probably finds himself a girlfriend every time a new yacht sails in. You're only a baby; you'll have to learn to be less trusting in future".'

By the time he'd finished, she remembered, the tears had been streaming down her face.

Now she managed to drag a smile of sorts from the depths of her anguish. 'He wanted to believe me, but he was too worried and his anger got the better of him. They both saw you as Casanova. I suppose it was because you were so good-looking.'

She glanced at the ring on her finger. Instead of love it was a symbol for revenge.

His voice broke roughly in on her thoughts. 'That's enough wallowing in the past. It's now I'm interested in. I want to eat. Let's have lunch. Come.'

He climbed out of the car.

She watched him go in a kind of terror. 'Christos!' she called after him. 'I can't. . .'

He lowered his head to look in at her. 'Can't? Can't what?'

'You know,' she whispered. 'How can we marry. . . without love?'

He tensed as at a body-blow. 'You'll do as I say,' he grated. 'I made the decision long ago. There is no going back. Get that straight. Come.' He grasped her by the arm and pulled her from the car. 'I have said you will redeem the past. Put on a smile. Our marriage is to be common knowledge. You will meet some of the people who performed the Greek chorus to our little drama those years ago. It is time to show ourselves to the public.'

CHAPTER SEVEN

WHEN Shelley stepped on to the pavement she realised they were outside one of the main hotels in Corfu. Christos leaned towards her, tucking her hand possessively in the crook of his arm.

'Come along, smile for the public. This is supposed to be a celebration.'

She winced. He must have ice in his veins. Had he no qualms about what they were doing? But then he was doing exactly what he wanted to do, wasn't he? He thought he had bought the right. No wonder he felt like celebrating.

As he led her up to the entrance of the restaurant she caught a glimpse of the lovely sight of the courtyard within, balconies rising in three tiers to an open roof, with a fountain playing in the middle. It was magnificent, a suitably romantic setting for making wedding plans, she thought bitterly.

He led the way through the revolving doors and they were met at once by the proprietor, who seemed to be an old friend of Christos and had obviously been expecting them. He made a rapid assessment of Shelley's cool English looks, then turned to Christos with a congratulatory smile. 'It is a great honour for me.' He was inclining his head to her. 'I gather this is a very special occasion.' He smiled again.

Shelley felt an irrational sense of betrayal that Christos had already hinted why they were here.

Stifling her emotions, she allowed her glance to travel round while the two men spoke together for a moment.

They were standing in an imposing inner court-yard, beautifully tiled in the traditional way, with a lot of frothy palms bursting out of large pots. It was obviously a fashionable rendezvous. Many beautiful and well dressed people were dining under the overhanging balconies, their elegant shapes reflected back from columns of Venetian glass.

They turned to observe the new arrivals, and she saw their own images—Christos's black head, his imposing figure, and her own blonde, very English looks—mirrored deep in the heart of the glass. It seemed appropriate to be seen like that, two elegant shapes of light and dark trapped in the cold mirror.

After a moment the two men turned and the proprietor himself began to usher them up a magnificent staircase to the table he had reserved for them in an exclusive corner on one of the balconies.

Christos put an arm lightly round her slender waist and with all the fond attention of a lover pretended to help her into her chair. Inwardly she cried at the sham of it all.

'You don't look happy,' he observed, putting his lips intimately against her ear as if bestowing a kiss on it.

'How can I be happy?' she responded low enough for the waiters not to overhear. 'It's beautiful here, but——' she bit her lip '—you know how I feel. It's all a pretence.'

He frowned and took his place opposite on one of the spiky gold chairs.

She picked up the heavy leather-bound menu and gazed uncomprehendingly at the dancing words. Her eyes were beginning to blur, but she pretended it was because she was having difficulty in making out the letters of the flowery italic script.

After a moment he leaned across. 'Perhaps I can help?' His black eyes inched expessionlessly over her face.

Silently she handed him the menu. When their fingers touched she nearly dropped it in her haste to avoid any physical contact. Again his black eyes inched over her face. He registered her response without comment.

Angry with herself, she fiddled with the heavy silver cutlery, longing to smash it on to the floor and say enough was enough, but she knew she couldn't.

Aware of the team of waiters ready to attend their every whim, she listened as he read the menu to her. Anyone listening to him would think how considerate he was being.

She avoided his glance and gazed instead into the courtyard, with its coming and going of lunch guests.

It seemed an age before the food appeared, although it wasn't actually very long. But Christos seemed to have withdrawn into himself.

He had chosen for them a selection of *maridhes*, followed by *dolmades, melidzanes* and *barbouni* — whitebait fried with fresh lemon as a starter, then mince in vine leaves, aubergine, and a succulent steamed red mullet accompanied by roasted pine kernels.

While the waiters were busy he leaned across the table. 'Try a little harder to accept the situation. This is the best restaurant on the island. You may as well resign yourself to pleasure.' He gave a hard laugh. 'I promise there will be much more to come. I am no puritan. I believe in the adage, "work hard and play hard". Now I am playing, and I intend to extract the maximum enjoyment from this situation.'

'Playing? Yes, you are! You are playing with me! I feel like a bird in a gilded cage.' She cast a furious glance round the restaurant.

'Perhaps you will discover there is pleasure to be had even in a gilded cage.' His expression was bleak.

'I doubt it!'

'Shelley, we cannot sit and snarl at each other all through lunch.' Injecting a deliberately affable tone into his words, he started to tell her something about Monasco Mercantile Marine, and the trials and tribulations of starting such an enterprise, and about the big break that had propelled him to the top.

'I always intended to get into shipping,' he told her. 'I tried to explain that to you all those years go, but I don't think you understood.'

She shook her head.

He went on, 'It is curious to ponder how little we knew about each other in those days. The difficulties and misunderstandings of language.' His eyes probed hers, as if to elicit a response.

The lump in her throat was too large to risk an answer. If he was trying to get to her by evoking the past she didn't want to listen.

As if reading her thoughts, he continued, 'I think I had the more difficult task. You were very shy. A most enigmatic beauty. But it should have been easy for you, as there was little to understand about me. I am still a very simple man.'

She gazed at him in astonishment.

'It is true,' he insisted, reading her expression. 'I appreciate beauty. I have a strong appetite for life. And I have always been ambitious. I like competing because I like winning.' The threat in his voice was unmistakable when he added, 'I always get what I want.'

Her blue eyes dropped to escape his gaze. He didn't have to remind her of that.

'I acquired my first boat when I was fourteen,' he told her, eyes becoming warm. 'I loved that old tub. It had an outboard more often in bits and pieces on the quay than not.' He lowered his head. 'No doubt you remember the mark-two version we used. It was usually in pretty much the same state.' He held her glance, as if willing her to summon up the memory. 'Do you remember the day we met?'

His tone was more intimate, but she couldn't tell whether it was intended to work on her feelings or not. He gave a feline smile that started deep in his eyes, and then she knew, and irrationally she felt a surge of excitement to realise it was deliberate.

He obviously had no difficulty in making his arrogant streak acceptable, especially when the caress in his voice was accompanied by a smile straight into her eyes. It made her feel she was the only person in the room. His glance lingered, direct and very personal.

It was just a cheap trick of seduction, she reminded herself. She managed a nod. 'I remember that day very well. We'd just sailed from Kérkira.'

Her voice sounded odd and she stopped, forcing herself to break the contact. But when he waited for her to continue in that careful, concerned, interested way it seemed to draw the words from her. 'Dad was in a state about coming into such a busy harbour. Everything went wrong. With the propeller out of action, we could have been pushed broadside on to the yachts already moored. I don't suppose it was the expense that worried him, more likely the humiliation of looking like a buffoon in front of everyone.'

She paused. His eyes were still fixed on hers. 'Luckily you must have guessed what was happening.'

'I saw him shouting at everybody and waving a boathook.'

They both laughed.

'You were like a marauding pirate, standing up in your boat, weaving past all the other boats. You did a bit of shouting yourself before you managed to persuade him to allow you to tie alongside.'

'Paula looked down her nose at my old tub. I remember her yelling at me to keep away. She must have thought I was going to scratch the paintwork.'

'Not good for apearances when you sail beneath the yacht club terrace.'

Again they both laughed, and their eyes met.

Recovering quickly, Shelley allowed her lashes to lower, cutting off that betraying exchange. He was deliberately trying to change her feelings towards him, but she wasn't going to allow him the satisfaction.

What she couldn't control was a vivid image of his bronzed torso dripping with water as he had emerged from under the boat with the line in one triumphant fist. He had looked so wonderful. She remembered his perfect body. The reckless brilliance of his smile. The way her heart had bumped.

Now she could feel his black eyes lingering over her face, and she wondered what he could remember about that first meeting. Had it meant anything at all to him?

She longed for a sign that there had been some corner in his heart for her, however small. In an effort to hide how deeply her emotions were running she pretended to be matter-of-fact. 'We were supposed to be on holiday, but Paula hated the yacht. When things went wrong she would say, "Find me in the yacht club, darling".'

Christos was still giving her all his attention, eyes now fixed to her lips.

She tried to ignore the feeling it aroused. 'My stepmother was always making new friends on the other yachts. Especially if they were "significant" enough.'

He raised his black brows. 'Significant?'

'Wealthy, titled or famous. Preferably all three.'

'None of which applied to me. . .at that time.' His expression became brooding and he tore his glance away, dark thoughts clouding his brow.

Evidently they got the better of his ability to switch on the charm, for his mouth tightened. She watched him take a sip of the Theotoki, a white wine from the local vineyards.

'I felt very sorry for you.' He gave a dismissive jerk of his head. 'Poor little rich girl.'

Shelley coloured violently.

He went on, 'I thought I might as well rescue the golden-haired princess. I was a romantic in those days.'

His black eyes swept her flushed cheeks without compassion. 'Whenever I came by your boat you were sitting on the deck alone with your head in a book.'

'I like reading,' she defended.

'You were surrounded by everything money could buy, not only beautiful clothes, but things like water-skis, sail-boards, snorkels, everything. All those toys and no one to play with. It was so sad.'

Her eyes brimmed suddenly at what his words meant. She bent her head and cut carefully at something on her plate without even seeing it. What was he trying to say? That he had turned up at the yacht every day out of pity? Deep inside she had clung on to the memory of those romantic excursions round the island. It hadn't seemed like pity. Even if, as he had proved, he had never loved her, she had at least thought he had seen her every day because he liked her.

Now he was telling her it had been pity.

She tried to swallow, but couldn't. There was a lump in her throat like a block of concrete.

She forced herself to speak through it. 'Wasn't it lucky for me you were there with so much time to spare? I must admit it was fairly dull without anybody of my own age to talk to. I was going to invite half a dozen schoolfriends along, but decided not to at the last minute.'

She tried to make her tone brittle enough to mask the swelling tide of emotion threatening to swamp her. He must never know how much she was hurting. His casual revelation of the truth was more destructive than any planned vendetta against her emotions.

Through blurring eyes she saw him give a hard smile. 'I'm glad I was able to keep you amused.'

Looking into his black pupils, she suddenly felt she was staring into a whirlpool. It frightened her to think what monsters were lying in wait to drag her below the surface.

Everything showed he remembered that summer as clearly as she did. The only difference was he saw things in another light, not as the romantic idyll she herself remembered.

The discovery destroyed any vestige of hope that in all the wreckage was a shared experience on which they could have built. It would have meant his intention to marry her had some redeeming feature of affection in it.

Obviously this was not the case.

She shivered at the prospect of the unloved years stretching ahead. How quickly his attempt to soften her resistance had given way to this black rage against the past. How could she survive?

The empty dishes had been cleared away without Shelley noticing and, summoned by a lift of Christos's head, a waiter brought a trolley to their table, crammed with sweetmeats.

She glanced briefly at the selection of mouth-watering delicacies displayed in their silver dishes.

'I remember you were fond of *baklava* in the old days.'

'I really don't want anything——' she began.

'I used to bring them for you fresh from the baker's.'

'Out of pity for me, I suppose?'

'And feed you morsels,' he concluded, voice lowering to a suggestive timbre. 'So how can you resist now?' He laughed pleasantly.

The waiter, evidently not understanding, began to indicate first one dish then another. 'There are *kataifi*, *trigono*, *galactobouri*——'

'Hey, Anastasius,' Christos addressed him, 'what about some *lukumadhes*? Then I'm sure the lady will surrender.'

The two men laughed as if sharing a joke, and Shelley felt furious with them.

'What are *lukumadhes*?' she asked, giving a cool glance at the waiter.

'They are the lightest waffles in the world, madam. They are created from a special flour ground on the island and from the finest Greek honey, collected from the wild flowers that clothe the mountain of the gods——'

Christos interrupted. 'She'll have a plate of those. And *baklava*, for the old days,' he added, lips betraying his cynicism. He noded to the waiter. 'And my usual to finish.'

To Shelley's vexation this turned out to be the tiny espresso she would rather have had and a thimbleful of fiery metaxa.

When they were alone again his black eyes probed her features. 'Tell me something. Did you see my attentions as the importuning of a ruffian who should have known better?' He paused. 'Or were you just a little bit flattered you had the most handsome boy on the island to show you the sights?'

She blushed. 'You know how I felt,' she replied in a choky voice.

He reached out and trapped her hand on the table. 'Tell me,' he commanded.

Her tone was guarded. 'I was glad.'

His watchful expression didn't alter, but his dark eyes were smouldering. 'Have you any idea what I felt then? Any idea?' he repeated, leaning forward.

Her breath stopped. 'How did you feel?'

There was a long silence.

She gazed across at him, willing him to put into words a hint of what she longed to hear.

His voice dipped. 'Didn't you guess?' He leaned forward to stare into her beautiful face. A corner of his mouth jumped. 'I wanted you. God, how I wanted you. I still want you.'

She searched his expression for some other sign, but even now his words, the look on his face, showed only the intensity of desire.

One of her hands lay palm upwards on the table, and he trailed his fingertips in a thrilling caress within its concave shape before gripping it powerfully in his own.

She could feel the energy of desire in every tiny contact. His fingers trembled over her own. He wanted her. Yes.

Then came the quiet warning to remind her of

what she must never forget. This wasn't love. It was the desire to possess. His motive was to avenge the past.

He squeezed her hand, and her muscles contracted in response.

'You have me. Here I am, trapped in my gilded cage,' she announced throatily, withdrawing her hand from its prison beneath his.

When they left the hotel the interested eyes of the remaining diners followed them to the doors. Shelley was aware of a wave of speculation as she glanced back. Christos gave no sign that he was aware of it, and, if he was, it was part of his scheme and nothing less than expected.

He slipped an arm round her wrist and walked her along the front to a busy café in the main square. It had striped green awnings, waiters in tails, table-cloths as stiff as boards, and an orchestra playing romantic ballads from a flower-decked dais. It looked like a fashionable rendezvous, with a small knot of people queuing for tables.

Christos was recognised at once and they were led at once to a table for two in a prominent position. All glances were again aimed in their direction. Shelley heard the whisper go round. 'Kiriakis,' she heard. Voices were diplomatically lowered.

Christos nodded to several groups of well dressed businessmen and their companions, but his attentiveness to Shelley dissuaded anyone from joining them.

Shelley noticed a face familiar from the movies, together with those of one or two others she felt she knew, but her attention was drawn irresistibly back to Christos. Plainly he had brought her here for a reason.

'These are the high-flying circles you inhabit these days, then?'

Registering an edge in her tone, he allowed his glance to laze over her face before asking, 'Doesn't it amuse you?'

'It surprises me. I didn't think you cared about such people. Or are we here to fulfill a more serious purpose?'

He gave his enigmatic smile. 'Quite right. Several of these people knew me in the old days.'

Fortunately a waiter brought a tray of drinks, and Shelley was saved from telling him what she felt at being exhibited like a prize purchase in front of everyone.

'I must show you my beach club soon. It's nearing completion. It's going to be a most exclusive resort. The best for the best. Club membership, of course.' His eyes were hooded, but there was suddenly some secret amusement in their depths.

She imagined a long list of international jet-setting celebrities. Looking round at the fashionable clientele in the café, she lifted her head in suspicion. 'Competition for the beach club Dad's building?'

He gave an amused shake of his hed. 'You're on the wrong track, my dear. My club is on the opposite side of the island. . .and membership is restricted to those under the age of eighteen! It's an adventure training centre for underprivileged children from all over Europe.'

He gave his rakish smile again, all the harshness

fleeing from his features, the dark eyes lightening when he saw her surprise. He added, 'I have a luxury holiday complex on the mainland to help subsidise it.'

A hint of arrogance tinged his smile. 'Paula would no doubt say, "Not bad for a peasant".'

Shelley felt an icy finger scud up her spine. The longer they were together, the more she realised how deeply that summer was burned into his memory.

Every ill considered remark had been stored and remembered. All the harsh insults flung at him in that final confrontation had been recorded. For someone whose English had only been rudimentary, it was quite a feat of memory.

They stayed only a short time in the café; just long enough, she thought furiously, for everyone to notice their presence. It was so obvious why he had brought her here.

A stream of people came over to be introduced before they left, and she noticed how lively were the conversations that followed their return to their respective groups.

Christos pulled back her chair. 'We've spent enough time here. Let's go.'

'Enough time to show everyone you have suc-ceeded in another one of your ambitions,' she said as cuttingly as she could. She stalked on ahead, making her way in a contained fury between the tables.

She was going to cure herself of her mad, ado-lescent infatuation for him, she vowed desperately as she looked back at him. All she had to do was survive until the danger was over and she could make her getaway.

Even Christos, bloody-minded though he was, would realise it was useless for them to remain married once his honour had been satisfied.

CHAPTER EIGHT

CHRISTOS fixed the date of the wedding with the priest, and rang to tell her so next morning. 'Three weeks from today.' He delivered the news with that familiar impatient tone. It conveyed what she already knew: there would be no reprieve.

He went on, 'You can tell Fitch I shan't object when he submits another application for running services under my land. The access road can open after the Easter break.'

'I'll tell him.' Her voice was subdued. There could be no sense of victory at having got things moving again.

Before he rang off he demanded to know whether she had informed her father of their wedding.

'Not yet,' she admitted nervously. 'He's ill, Christos. I daren't upset him.'

She decided to speak to Malcolm first, before making the dreaded call to St Lucia. She didn't know if Malcolm had got around to telling her father there was trouble at the Corfu site. Her hand slid over the cold plastic, then, taking her courage in both hands, she lifed the receiver and began to dial Malcolm's home number in Surrey.

She got straight through.

'Shelley! How's it going?' He sounded desperate. 'Made any progress?'

Progress? she thought ironically. It depends how

118

you look at it. 'You'll be relieved to know I've managed to come to an arrangement with Mr Kiriakis. The men will be back at work next week, straight after the Greek Easter.'

'Thank heavens!' He gave an uncharacteristic whoop of triumph. 'I can't tell you how relieved I am. Well done.' His delight and relief were palpable. She had saved the project, and she could tell he was almost dancing with joy. 'So are you coming straight back or do you want to stay on a few days to perfect that tan?'

Annoyed that he hadn't bothered to ask about the 'arrangement' she'd had to make, she said, 'That's another thing I have to tell you, Malcolm. I won't be coming back. At least. . .' she paused '. . .not until after my wedding.'

There was a long pause.

'This is rather sudden, I mean, are you serious?' He seemed to be floundering for the right thing to say. 'I'd no idea this was in the offing. Is it to some chap you've met out there?'

When she told him, there was another pause.

'Well, well. . . I suppose love can strike you women like a bolt from the blue,' he opined. 'I would never have expected anything like this from you, though, Shelley. You always seemed so level-headed.' He was recovering fast, while she herself was still having trouble getting used to the idea.

'Well, there it is,' she affirmed.

She returned the receiver to its rest. Now she had to ring Paula.

This was going to be the toughie, she thought, biting her lower lip. Fingers trembling, she started

dialling the complicated number that would connect
her to the beach hotel in St Lucia where her stepmother was staying. Lines out to the island were
often busy, but she got through to the desk without
much trouble. When they tried to contact Paula's
suite, however, they were unable to get a reply.

'Hi, caller,' said the receptionist in friendly fash-
ion. 'I understand Mrs Burton is out sightseeing
today. May I take a message?'

'No, it's all right. I'll call later.' So much for
Florence Nightingale, she thought. Obviously Paula
had tired of the role already. Replacing the receiver,
she rang the exclusive St Lucia convalescent home
where her father had gone to recuperate after his
heart attack two months earlier in London. She
spoke to the director.

'He still needs complete rest,' he told her. When
he discovered it was his patient's daughter he was
talking to a more reassuring note came into his
voice. 'He has been burning the candle at both ends
for many years. But be assured, Miss Burton, he is
out of danger so long as there is nothing to upset
him.'

Shelley heaved a sigh of relief after she replaced
the phone for this third time. Looking on the bright
side, she supposed that at least Dad was in good
hands and improving, and she had got the building
project on the move again. But the thought that
Christos was holding her to ransom made her anger
rise like a thick tide. She got up and went into the
kitchen.

Anna was preparing a salad when she went in,
little Theodora grizzling in her mother's skirts, and

Anna gave a smile of relief when she saw her. 'Now my little monster will smile again,' she exclaimed. She gave Shelley a grin. 'Always it is, "Mama, I want Shell-ee". I tell her, Shelley is busy lady, no time for play. But she not listen.'

'It's all right!' Shelley scooped the little girl into her arms. 'I'll take her outside to play.' Chanting, 'Sacks of coal! Sacks of coal!' she carried the at once gurgling two-year-old over her shoulder into the garden. It was a relief to be given some respite from all her problems. The three older children descended on her as soon as she appeared and she had to do 'sacks of coal' four times over until they all flopped down exhausted on the grass.

Niko and Alexei immediately sat on her tummy, and the two girls vied at plaiting the long strands of Shelley's hair. She lay back, their gentle fingers tugging at the golden locks they found so fascinating, and decided she had better tell Spyro and Anna about the wedding.

Little Theodora tickled her face and sat down, plop, on her chest, her chubby fingers gripping tightly to one of the tiny plaits her older sister had made. '*Hrissos! Hrissos!*' she lisped in her baby voice.

'What is she saying?' Shelley asked Niko, recognising the word from the day before, when she'd met Christos's mother.

'She say "gold"—very pretty,' Niko told her, proud of his knowledge. 'She like have gold hair also.'

'She's simply perfect as she is,' remarked Shelley, cuddling the little girl in her arms.

She was laughing as the other children fell on top of her, demanding cuddles too, when a black shape suddenly loomed over her. Looking up, she felt a constriction in her throat, then her limbs froze into the position they already held. The sound of the children's piping voices faded as the last person she expected to see stood looking down at her. She glowered up at him.

He was eyeing her as if he couldn't believe what he saw, the black eyes expressionless, assessing this scene of domesticity, Shelley with babies in her arms. Then his glance touched every feature of her tousled appearance. She put up a hand and felt the little plaits sticking out at all angles. Her face reddened. No doubt there would be scathing comments about her appearance again, but, to her surprise, although he observed the gesture he didn't make any remark, merely saying, 'I rang you straight back, but your line was engaged. Did you take it off the hook?' he questioned.

'Of course not!' She struggled on to her elbows. 'It's not my home anyway, Christos. It's Spyro's.'

His lips were set in a straight line. 'Are you busy?'

She sat right up, struggling in a heap of arms and legs, but still clutching the little one to her. 'What does it look like?'

'Ambiguous.' His eyes glimmered for a moment. 'I wanted to ask you to invite Spyro and his wife to dinner. We were at school together.'

'Yes,' she said stiffly, 'he said he remembered you.'

He continued to look at her.

'Come for a drive.'

'I can't. I said I'd help Anna with the food. She's preparing a special spit-roast lamb, and friends are coming round to celebrate.'

'Yes, it's our tradition on Easter Sunday. The lamb symbolises the Lamb of God.'

'You'll understand why I can't come with you, then?'

Just then Spyro came into the garden. 'Christos!'

To Shelley's blank astonishment the two men flung their arms round each other and proceeded to clap each other on the back as if they were long-lost brothers.

She gazed at them both, blue eyes disbelieving, trying to understand what they were saying to each other, but she couldn't follow it; they were speaking far too rapidly. Eventually remembering her presence, Spyro turned to her with a beaming smile.

'Anna tell me he is here. I could not believe it.' He turned back to Christos. 'We must all now speak English for Shelley's sake. You will of course eat with us.'

To give Christos credit, thought Shelley grudgingly, he seemed rather embarrassed at being invited into the household with such instant generosity, and she wondered if he was suffering a twinge of conscience at the thought of how he had nearly done Spyro out of his job, for Colin Burton would have had heads rolling right, left and centre if he'd discovered what had been going on.

Anna came out just then and, after a shy look at Christos, spontaneously added her invitation to that of her husband. 'It will be very simple,' she explained. 'Like old days. We would like you very much to eat with us.'

Christos gave Shelley a brief, ironic glance, as if to challenge her to voice her objections, but she merely tossed her head and pretended to be more interested in the children.

'Have you told them?' The dark head bent close when Anna and Spyro went back indoors, Anna to continue her preparations, Spyro to fix the drinks.

'Told them what?' she replied, playing for time.

'Don't be awkward. I mean about our wedding.'

'No, not yet.'

'I thought maybe that's why they'd invited me to stay.'

'I haven't an earthly why they invited you. They're inviting hordes of people.'

'I propose we make a formal announcement before the meal, then.'

Stifling her instant response to this, she said, 'It beats me why Spyro greeted you like a long-lost brother when he knows you were the one behind all our trouble——'

'He will have no hard feelings because he will understand,' Christos cut in.

'Understand? Understand what?'

'That you were the foreign girl involved in that scene nine years ago.'

Trembling, Shelley picked up one of the children who'd been swinging familiarly on his arm. 'You're going to tell him?'

'I must say,' he went on before she could object,

'it's good to see you have a maternal instinct striving to get out.'

'Buried under the hard-boiled exterior, you mean?'

He angled his head, and there was a glint in his dark eyes, a splinter of gold, warm and inviting. 'No, I meant because I like children and intend to have a large family.'

Outrage melted at once to a strange yearning. Confused by her own reaction, she asked, 'Won't I have any say in the matter?' Her voice sounded husky.

'I pray you'll feel the same way.' His eyes smouldered into hers.

By now the children were clamouring to be played with, and Shelley grabbed it as an opportunity to get away from him.

The barbecue started at midday and went on late into the afternoon and evening. As Christos had already told her, he wanted to take it as an opportunity to announce their wedding.

Shelley watched him as he rose and proceeded to make a preliminary speech. He held everyone's attention.

'And so,' he continued, 'to prove that the reputation of Corfu as an island of love is still intact, it was here where we met.' Christos paused and shot her a triumphant look. 'And Shelley fulfilled my secret dreams and agreed to marry me. I hope you will join in wishing us long life and happiness together. A toast to my beautiful future bride.'

He brought her fingers to his lips and while she

shot daggers at him from beneath her lashes he sat down beside her amid genuine applause. Then the congratulations began to pour in. It seemed a remarkably popular announcement. Shelley, smiling through gritted teeth, was kissed on both cheeks by everybody present, her silence no doubt taken as a sign that she was too overwhelmed with joy to speak.

Christos had worked hard to gain such a reaction, she considered, coming out with a lot of flowery stuff about the history of Corfu and Illyrian princesses and heavens knew what else. He certainly had the gift of the gab. No wonder he had made such a success of his relatively humble origins.

And how he'd taken everyone in too, claiming it was love at first sight nine years ago! That had gone down very well. The good red Kastellani wine had put everyone in a sentimental mood. They seemed ready to believe anything. She herself seemed to be about the only one who was stone-cold sober.

It was late now. Anna was heading towards the house, a sleepy child in each hand. She made her way after her. 'Let me put them to bed, Anna. You've been slaving in the kitchen most of the day. At least go and enjoy the fruits of so much hard work.'

'Would you do that, Shelley? Is so kind. You know what to do?'

'I'm sure they'll tell me if I don't get it right!'

'*Parakalo*. And Shelley, I so happy for you. Is very good man. Forgive for what I say. Is good man now. I not know you are foreign girl he left home for. True love always win!'

Assured that Shelley had forgiven her her comment about watching Christos from the safety of closed shutters, she bent to kiss both children fondly goodnight and allowed Shelley to lead them off.

After she'd settled them Shelley lingered in the hallway, reluctant to rejoin the convivial group round the barbecue, relishing the liquid silence indoors that gave her an opportunity to think about this other side to Christos. Could she imagine him as the father of her children? The frightening thing was, she could. He would be a wonderful father.

Her ruminations were cut short when the subject of her thoughts came shouldering in through the garden door. 'Are you all right?' he demanded.

'I'm fine.' Her voice sounded strained.

She gave a shaky laugh. Just to see him made her feel weak with longing.

'Why are you standing alone here in the dark?' His voice penetrated the night with the softness of velvet. Somewhere a piano was playing, echoing in a distant room. The bittersweet refrain made her feel like crying. Why couldn't all those things he had said just now be true? Love at first sight. For all time. Why couldn't the gods let him love her?

Angry at letting him bring her to the point of tears, she scrubbed at her face in the dark. When she thought her voice was under control she asked, 'What was that story about the princess? It went down well. Everybody seemed to know it.'

His warm chuckle came out of the darkness. 'It is an old legend of the island. Lanassa was a princess from Illyria who came to Corfu to mend her broken heart.'

'Oh, really?' She was regretting this already.

'Oh, yes,' he agreed mildly. 'But when she reached here she met the handsome prince Denetius. Shortly after, she sent him a proposal of marriage.'

'I didn't know they behaved like that in those days.'

'Don't doubt it. Strong women have always done as they pleased.'

'Did this Denetius accept the strong woman's proposal?'

'He certainly did.' His warm laughter came out of the darkness. 'Of course, he had already signed a non-aggression pact with her father, so it made sense.'

She gave a croaky laugh. 'I see there's no mention of love in this story. Quite appropriate in the circumstances.'

Unable to bear it any longer, she made her way blindly across the hall towards the doorway. His hands seemed to reach out for her, but she pushed them aside, slipping out into the garden and rejoining the others near the glowing spit.

Throughout the full three weeks before the wedding the conventions were strictly obeyed. She remained chaperoned at the house with Spyro and Anna.

As she was due for some holiday-leave, there were no problems with leaving things under Malcolm's control in London.

Christos seemed ferociously busy. He never seemed to stop, and she got a good idea why he was so phenomenally successful. He was often away on business, first Tokyo, then LA, then back to Hong

Kong. On their rare meetings when he touched down between flights he did little more than bestow a chaste kiss on her lips before driving away to his next assignment.

'I want an end to all this travel. After our wedding it will be different,' he told her one evening. 'I am not one of these men content to see their wives only at weekends. Also,' he reminded, 'I want to get to know my children. I don't intend to be an absentee father.'

She stifled a nervous laugh. His words were outrageous enough — never in one place for more than a day or two at a time, how was he ever going to change?

Worse was the reminder that he wanted them to have lots of babies.

It made the reality of what they were embarking on strike home yet again, and it shattered her vague expectation that he only wanted the show of a wedding to satisfy his honour. Obviously it was marriage in the fullest sense he was bent on.

Day by day the tension rose. She was only glad no one who knew her well would be present at the wedding. They would read her feelings all over her face — her fear, and her despair that there was no question of love involved.

She eventually managed to contact Paula. 'I want you to prepare Dad for the news when he's well enough, Paula, make it seem less of a shock,' she told her. She prayed her stepmother would try to be sympathetic, but by the tone of their conversation she feared the worst. At least Paula agreed not to break the news until the doctors gave her the go-ahead.

There had been no further word from St Lucia. It was breaking Shelley's heart to think her father wouldn't be giving her away at the ceremony.

The days dragged. Each night seemed like a year as she tossed and turned between the crisp sheets in the virginal blue and white room at Spyro's.

Anna helped her choose a simple white silk shift as a wedding-gown, its simplicity a foil for the magificent full-length veil of old lace crafted long ago by Christos's great-great-grandmother.

When he brought it round to the house a few days before the wedding he handed it to her in a leather container, much battered, but adorned in faded gold Greek letters. By now Shelley could read the script. It was the name of the family, Kiriakis. It seemed strange and alien. She found it difficult to imagine that this soon would be her own name by right of law.

He insisted that she open the lid and take out the contents.

An aroma of old lavender clung to the lace as she lifted it from its box. Stretching up her arms, she held it so that it fell in a trail of gossamer threads across the floor, every stitch worked to perfection in a pattern of twining flowers and birds.

'It's beautiful, Christos.' There was a catch in her throat. 'It's quite lovely.' She allowed the fine threads to run through her fingers, touching them delicately to inspect the ins and outs of the pattern. Ironically, there were hearts among the flowers, and tiny cherubs, portents for the future.

* * *

The ceremony that made them man and wife took place in the privacy of a tiny Byzantine chapel in a remote valley in the hills.

It was a very private ceremony. Anna was in attendance with the children. Her two boys were unrecognisable in white silk trousers and traditional baggy shirts with black shoes you could see your face in, and her little bridesmaid daughters looked sweet with coronets of white rosebuds on their dark curls.

As Shelley stepped down from the wedding car with Spyro to give her away, little Theodora toddled forward to offer a posy of wild flowers, then scurried back in a flurry of lace petticoats to the others.

Most important guest was Christos's mother, frail and proud in black watered silk, attended by a distant cousin or two. Their faces turned to watch this foreign bride as she hesitated at the door of the chapel.

Shelley's glance flew the length of the nave. Her first view of the man who was to become her husband was the back of his black head. He stood beside the priest at the simple altar framed between the sun-washed arches of the ancient building. There was a smell of beeswax and honey.

Clutching her cascade of flowers, she took a hesitant step down the aisle. Then Christos turned and their eyes met, and she faltered. She drew in a sharp breath with the shock of seeing him.

He looked incredibly handsome in traditional dinner-jacket and white tie, with a single white rose in his buttonhole. The immaculate black wings of his hair aroused a tender longing in her to reach out and touch. There was something oddly reticent about him as his eyes met hers.

Despite everything, she yearned to touch. To be touched by him.

Yet he had forced her into this ceremony, and it was all a sham.

Heart breaking, she drifted towards his outstretched hand. The space between them seemed to consume them, the beautiful veil trailing behind her, the white slippers making soft sounds like little sighs over stones worn bronze with age. He reached for her hand, gripping it wordlessly.

Knowing she was trapped, she bowed her head beneath the folds of lace. The intricate ritual began to unfold. All the time the pressure of his fingers on her wrist was concealed beneath the veil.

Surely, she prayed, during the beauty and solemnity of the service Christos could not remain unmoved by the vows of love he was making?

Her fingers trembled as Christos placed the simple gold band next to the betrothal ring of green and blue and red. He bent to kiss her, and she knew it was a moment she would remember till the day she died.

In showers of rose petals, with good wishes resounding on all sides, they eventually made their way towards the waiting open-top cars to take them back into Kérkira for the reception.

But just before they left the precincts of the hilltop chapel, Christos's mother caught her by the wrist and said in slow, clear Greek, 'This —' she fingered

Shelley's wedding ring '—this would make my husband very happy.' She squeezed Shelley's hand.

The moment was over in an instant, but the words echoed and re-echoed in Shelley's mind.

Minutes later, her long veil blown in a joyful curve by the speed with which the driver took them back down the valley, she felt a stoic smile come to her face. Of course Mr Kiriakis would have been happy. He would have been very happy indeed—to witness the day when the honour of the Kiriakises was at last publicly restored!

A cold knife twisted in Shelley's heart. She had just been married to the one man in the world she loved with body and soul. She should have felt as radiant as she no doubt looked. But how could she feel an iota of happiness? Her love was not returned. The man sitting beside her was acting a part; it was sham, all sham.

And the worst was yet to come.

First there was a convivial wedding feast at the best hotel on the island for those not invited to the private ceremony.

Champagne and flowers, everything his wealth could provide, was there. Yet it floated before her eyes like a dream.

As soon as the toasts were made Christos bent his dark head. 'We are going to get away as soon as we can.' His voice was hoarse.

Almost too soon to avoid gossip, he whisked her away in his Rolls, driving straight to the quay where his black and silver motor yacht was berthed.

Still in her wedding-gown, she took his arm as he

helped her down from the flower-decked car on to the pontoon. A party of revellers had followed, catching up with them in time to witness Christos scoop the slender body of his protesting bride into his arms and carry her boldly in all her silks and lace across the gangplank to the yacht.

There were cheers, and flowers were pelted across the water to land on deck. A breeze caught her long veil and lifted it in a swirl of lace, and as Christos held her it drifted down, enveloping them in its perfumed folds.

In the secrecy behind the veil she felt his lips, hot and hungry, seeking hers. The cries of the revellers faded. She became conscious of nothing but Christos.

CHAPTER NINE

CHRISTOS held her body against his as she slid to her feet, and she could feel his hard, aroused male shape through the thin silk of her wedding-gown. His hands slid over her hips hungrily, like a portent of what was to come.

Reluctantly he released her. 'I have to start the engines. With no one on board you'll have to help. Go and change while I cast the lines off.'

His desire was palpable, an inner fury, eating into him.

She went below to change, nervously pushing open the door of the state-room and peering inside. It was decked with flowers, orchids in profusion, and bottles of champage in silver buckets.

But her eyes were drawn like magnets towards the double bed. She was shaking as she made her way over to it. On the sumptuous oyster satin counterpane one of the staff had laid out her new nightgown, an expensive sheath of silk and lace, a wedding gift among many others Christos had showered on her in the last few days.

But the time for that wasn't yet. Trembling with nerves, she stripped to her underwear and climbed into a pair of shorts, topping them with a blue and white cotton sweater. With her blonde hair caught up in a silk square trimmed with red and blue anchors she went back on deck.

Christos let his glance trail over her. With an effort he forced his glance from her long, tanned legs. 'Go on to the foredeck. I want you to start bringing up the anchor.'

He went below for a moment and came back dressed in a pair of white drill trousers and a T-shirt; then she watched him climb on to the bridge, taking the steps athletically two at a time.

The powerful engines began to growl as he prepared to move off. Activating the automatic winch with her bare feet, she twisted her head to keep an eye out for his signal.

Christos was staring down at her. His black eyes didn't leave her face as he opened the throttle. There was an unspoken line of communication between them, feverish in its intensity. It sent violent shivers of expectation rippling up and down her body. She knew what it meant.

Time seemed to unfold with desperate slowness. Everything seemed to take an age. Moment by moment they went through the routine necessary to get them to sea. As soon as he saw her head pass the wheelhouse he unleashed more power until the engines roared. Then his face became fixed in concentration as he piloted them out of the harbour.

Shelley stayed in the stern where she could watch him, as, bracing hard against the big chrome wheel, he spun it masterfully between tanned, sensitive fingers to every shift of the sea's motion. She imagined them in the night to come, touching her with the same assurance.

The muscles of his thighs flexed and relaxed, the

compact strength fighting the sea as it tried to fling the boat out of control.

She dragged her glance away. It made her tremble to think of that black will focused solely on her. Thoughts fused in one stream of dread and yearning for the night ahead. That he didn't feel anything like love for her haunted her with sickening persistence.

When the roar of the engines dropped to a soft snarl Christos swung down from the bridge. She gave a start to find him suddenly standing beside her.

He bent down and touched one of her cheeks with the back of his hand.

'Don't you want to know where we're going to spend our first night?' he demanded. A lock of black hair flopped over his forehead. He pushed it back and regarded her with a critical lift of his brows. 'Or does it not interest you?'

She shrugged her shoulders. 'Anywhere is fine by me.' What did it matter when he didn't love her?

He told her, 'Tonight I make the choice. All nights after this are yours.'

He rested a hand on her shoulder. 'If you want to visit Venice, we do that. South to the islands, yes. Down through the Gulf to Athens. Across to Italy. To Rimini, Brindisi. Anywhere. Yours is the choice.'

'It sounds like the executioner asking the condemned man what he wants for breakfast,' she whispered. Why couldn't he see it didn't matter?

His eyes went cold; then, stifling a snarl, he thrust out one hand and ran it over the top of her soft hair, sliding his fingers inside her head square and ripping it to one side so that her hair tumbled free around her shoulders.

His other hand brushed underneath her chin, lifting it and caressing the silky skin as he did so. 'Why so miserable? Is martyrdom not to your taste after all?'

A spasm of emotion shook through him, and she felt his fingers tremble. He gazed long and deep into her eyes.

She tried to drop her glance, but he lifted her chin further, so that she was forced to look up and submit herself to his piercing attack. Was it rage she saw in the black depths?

After a long, confused moment he rasped, 'When I saw your face set in such an image of misery all through the ceremony I nearly called it off. I saw it is hateful to you to find yourself shackled to me.'

Her lips trembled. 'But I could not,' he went on. 'Our names were linked once before and now they are linked again. This time they will remain so forever.'

He let his hand drop, as if to touch her was painful.

'Come. Let's get the anchor down and switch off the engine. My staff have left a meal for us below. After tonight we shall have to fend for ourselves. The gallery is fully provisioned.' He turned and went back to the controls. Knowing what was expected, she made her way forward to activate the anchor mechanism. Till now she had scarcely looked at her surroundings, but as she stood in the bows she lifted her head.

They were in a narrow bay surrounded on three

sides by towering walls of silvery granite. There were no houses of any sort. It was a honeymooner's paradise, secluded and remote. The only sign of life was a couple of caiques, splashes of red and blue. They were drawn up next to each other on an arc of empty beach.

When the engines fell silent she heard the hiss of surf on the ledges of rock, and the whispering trill of cicadas on the headland. A slumbering tranquillity seemed to hold the entire bay in its thrall. It was a place made for lovers. But its magical beauty only added to the pain of her bleeding heart as it gushed relentlessly from the wounds of unreturned love.

When they were securely anchored for the night he prowled towards her along the deck. She flinched as he lifted one hand to her shoulder. His eyes inched over her trembling limbs.

'Cold?' he asked.

She shook her head.

His eyes glittered. 'I see.' He nodded with grim satisfaction. 'Have patience. This is no ordinary occasion. It cannot be hurried. It is long waited for. Much planning has gone into its preparation. My chef has expended his best efforts for our pleasure. We must show our gratitude and dress for dinner.'

To her surprise he led the way below.

The state-room seemed to shrink in size as they both changed out of their day clothes.

Shelley tried to avert her glance as Christos stripped without embarrassment to a pair of brief boxer shorts. His physique was impressive, tougher and more powerful than she remembered. The wild silk of his shorts clung to every clearly defined muscle, and another secret glance revealed the flat knotted stomach, hard thighs, perfect laterals, every muscle in his back rippling as he eased his white dinner shirt over his shoulders.

The urge to reach out and run her fingers over the sheen of bronze clothing them welled up in her without warning, and she had to fight to suppress it. Seeming to sense what she was thinking, he suddenly lifted his head, catching her look before she could stifle the open desire on her face.

In a moment he was beside her. He reached out and his mouth claimed hers in a plundering kiss.

'How do you expect me to keep away from you for a second longer when you look at me that way?' he growled close by her ear. 'I should take you here, this moment, now, savagely, without formality, like a barbarian. . .' He broke off, observing her shuddered response. 'But——' he gave an arctic smile '——we are not barbarians. First we will eat.' His eyes brooded over her flushed face for a moment. She felt a trembling breath release itself.

He turned back to the dressing-table and picked up his bow-tie, deftly fastening it as he made for the door. 'Finish dressing. Then come up on deck.'

He left the room, and she was thrown into confusion by the dismissive way he had turned from her.

If only she didn't long for him. Wanting and not wanting him were a feverish battle inside her. She fought against the overwhelming tide of conflicting emotions and forced herself to think of more mundane things.

For this, their first night, she had chosen a sleeveless deep red silk-jersey evening dress, its simple

lines offering no clue to its intricate design. As it
slipped over her head she felt it cling to her slender
shape as if it had been painted on. When she took a
step it flowed with her movements, caressing her
breasts, her thighs, with the sensuality of rare silk.
The colour perfectly complemented her soft blonde
hair, highlighting its silvery glints. She stepped into
a pair of high-heeled sandals and slid a couple of
silver bangles on to her wrist.

When she went to join Christos he was standing
on deck, his back to her, a glass in one hand, looking
across the strait. The dark waters glimmered with
the last lights of sunset, while around him the
flaming gold of the Ionian sun sank in primitive
splendour.

'Christos?'

He turned abruptly, as if not expecting to see her
so soon. On his face was an expression of something
inscrutable. It seemed he was looking at her for the
first time.

Wordlessly he put his glass down and held out
both hands to her. She found herself walking blindly
towards him, longing to believe in his love's awak-
ening, the dull pain hammering behind her ribs
telling her it wasn't so.

He seemed determined to observe the proprieties
to the bitter end. A pre-dinner glass of champagne
on deck was accompanied by polite small talk, and
she marvelled at his self-control. Didn't he feel this
urgent need to abandon all pretence now they were
alone? It was torture to have to submit to this
deliberate drawing out of the moment before the

final surrender. Perhaps he was having second thoughts, she wondered in wild surmise.

She was aware of every accidental and not so accidental touch, his fingers brushing her arm as they went below, the pressure of his thigh against hers, the heat of his palm on her waist as he helped her into a chair, his black eyes hooded, probing her, never leaving her for more than a moment, yet never revealing his own dark thoughts at what they were about to do.

She tasted nothing of the chef's inspired creations, so acutely conscious was she of the changing nuances of his glance. It was as if some parallel electric current ran between them, crackling with the energy of desire.

'You have never looked more lovely, Shelley,' he opined as the meal drew to a close, 'your soft hair framing your face, eyes more beautiful than anything in creation. They make me think of the skies of heaven.'

His voice was hoarse, an intimate growl. 'That dress,' he whispered. 'It makes me want to cut those flimsy straps and see it slither to the floor.'

He leaned back in his chair and regarded her silently for a moment with his black eyes, then he said, 'Have you considered how difficult the last three weeks have been for me?'

When she lifted her head he went on, 'Not to touch you, not to claim what I desire above all else.' He leaned forward. 'Was it difficult for you, too?'

She couldn't trust herself to speak, aware of the deliberate promise in his black eyes.

'No answer?' His mouth hardened.

He reached out, his grip tightening round her wrist, and pulled her towards him across the table. When he pulled her closer still the movement sent one of the champagne goblets toppling to the floor, where it shattered in an expensive shower of crystal.

Christos paid no heed and merely cupped one hand around the back of her head to bring her face within range of his mouth. She felt it crush down in a sudden savage spasm of desire, his jaw forcing her mouth to open to allow the instant entry of his seeking tongue.

Fragile china and silver cutlery were swept crazily on to the floor after the broken goblet as he dragged her hungrily towards him and she felt the fingers of his other hand circle one bare shoulder, then slide with unstoppable insistence inside the flimsy silk of the scarlet dress.

His fingers closed over the warmth and softness of her breast, teasing and moulding the instantly proud peak, coaxing a gasp from her he was quick to observe.

Standing, he pulled her to her feet, and slid the straps of her dress down over her shoulders, so that it sank to the floor in a sigh of silk, as he'd promised, leaving her almost nude in front of him, save for the wisp of a virginal white tanga, so small that it was hardly there at all.

Now that she was revealed at last to his gaze his eyes inched over her nakedness with a look of intense desire. He groaned, bending to rest his lips at the base of her throat. He took her possessively in his arms, trailing his strong, sensitive fingers over her creamy skin. Nothing had prepared her for the

sudden clamour of excitement that rang right
through her.

'So warm, so wanting,' he murmured deep in his
throat, tones thickening even more as he murmured
words of Greek she couldn't understand. He ran his
hands possessively over her curving hips until they
came to the soft silk V, then, bending, he thrust his
black head between her breasts, lifting his dazed
glance to her face before dipping again to graze her
soft curves. He drew her unresisting body towards
him, arching her so as to bring the thrust of his hard
arousal against the silk gold of her spread thighs.

With the delirium of need mounting at the speed
of a tidal wave and engulfing her blindly in it, she
gasped his name, clinging frantically to a token
resistance to stave off the final surrender. At the
back of her mind was the idea that if she did not give
in she would be able to survive his lack of love. But
her resistance crumbled at once. This was her wedding night and she was married to the man she
adored, and all she desired was to surrender to the
powerful need to love him.

Something deep inside unleashed itself, sending
both hands plunging recklessly into the thickness of
his hair, dragging his head hard against her aching
breasts. His lips fastened hotly on her erect nipples,
exciting them to yield further fantasies of pleasure,
his fingers inching over her naked limbs, inviting her
long, tanned legs to wrap involuntarily around him
while her head dropped back in total surrender.

Christos gave a muffled curse, taken by surprise
at her sudden active participation in the seduction
he had embarked upon. 'Yes, yes, angel,' he mut-

tered against the side of her head. 'But not here. Come with me.'

Breathing deeply, he carried her through the narrow door of the main cabin and down the corridor into the opulent state-room. Lowering her on to the oyster satin bedspread, his own male bulk followed at once in a crushing fall.

He spread her limbs, running his hands in a feverish caress over their quivering shape, words of desire whispering into her ear as he lowered his head. The hot touch of his mouth closed over her own before it moved in a trail of kisses down her neck to the hardening peak and she cried out with the unfamiliar pleasure he aroused.

Slowly his fingers began to inch her tanga down over her thighs. She moved to make it easier, reaching out to touch the hard contours of his chest in the opening of his shirt, then she watched as he quickly undressed. His nakedness took her breath away. She wanted him, every part of him, his body hot and vibrant against her own, and she brought up both hands to run them hungrily over the muscles of his back, over his hard thighs, his rough chest.

He gazed down at her, eyes smouldering, more intensely dark than ever before, then he bent to tease his tongue over the flat plane of her stomach, caressing and kissing her till she could feel darts of flame shooting through her, and she felt herself press more longingly against him.

With each of his palms cupping her full curves he entered her with all the sensuality in his power. A gasp of pain issued from her throat, but it vanished as she began to move beneath him, instinctively matching her arching rhythm to his own, yielding and reaching for him in alternate spasms to match the thirst and withdrawal of his male force.

In seconds she was clawing randomly at the hard muscles of his back as he arched over her. In her mind hammered a silent plea that he would now say he loved her, but soon even that thought was abandoned in the swift, final, exultant release, and she gave a cry, sobs of pleasure gasping haphazardly through her shaking form.

Too confused by feelings she had never even imagined, she failed to notice the shocked look on his face as he stroked back the tangled fronds of hair from her moist brow.

A long night of pleasure followed, and if she could have had one wish it would have been that it could never end. But eventually they fell asleep in each other's arms, satiated, sticky limbs wrapped protectively around each other as the dawn began to break. It felt like heaven to feel his heavy arms, his thighs weighted with sleep trapping her beneath them. She turned her mouth to rest it against his sleeping brow.

Love, she breathed so softly so she wouldn't wake him, love, love me.

She awoke next morning to find herself sprawled naked and alone across the bed.

Sunlight precisely placed itself across the undersheet in two circles, streaming in through the open portholes. Somewhere she could smell coffee.

Then she remembered how completely she had given herself to him through the night.

He could have no doubt that his revenge was now complete.

The chinking of crockery aroused her attention and her eyes fluttered open to see Christos ducking in through the cabin door. He wore nothing but a towel, startlingly white against his dark body. There was a silver tray balanced in both hands.

'*Kalimera, Kyria Kiriakis.*'

His use of her married name reminded her of what he had said to her yesterday. 'Our names were linked once before and now they are linked again. This time they will remain so forever.'

He sat down beside her on the bed. When his towel slipped, he pushed it to one side, unashamed at displaying his naked body to her gaze. She couldn't help the way her glance swooped with renewed desire over his wonderful body. It glowed with life. She longed to hold him again and to feel his desire quicken inside her. She flushed and averted her head.

Placing the tray on top of the bedside cabinet, he bent to place a kiss on her soft mouth.

'Your thoughts are very plain to read. I think you intend to give me no rest.' His fingers skimmed a teasing path down the elegant length of her spine. He drew her against his hot body, but she rolled over, burying her face in the pillows.

She felt his hot breath on the back of her neck.

He turned her over with the care of somebody revealing some shy wild creature. 'Are you happy?'

Happy, she thought, when I love you so much? She tried to bury her face again, afraid he could read her feelings in her eyes. But he held her beneath him, his dark eyes only inches from her own.

'I want you to be happy even if it is a gilded cage,' she heard him murmur.

Her blonde hair lay in trails across her face, a veil she hoped he wouldn't penetrate.

Strand by strand he uncovered her, pressing his lips against each flushed inch of skin as he revealed it, until she was totally revealed to his gaze. He pressed his lips against her temple and whispered, 'Tell me something about last night. Why did you wait so long?'

Squirming to get away, she longed to confess. Because of you. There was always the image of you, reminding me what love was like.

But she couldn't find the words; they were too dangerous, too confessional, ultimately too humiliating to admit to the man who had cold-bloodedly engineered her into his bed. Her thoughts remained where they were, embedded in silence. It would be the final defeat to admit them.

She gave a little laugh and glanced away, ignoring his question, and made a move to get dressed.

That morning began an idyll. It was the perfect honeymoon, at least on the surface, for they simply followed the whims of the day with no pre-set plan. Neither of them seemed to want to leave the isolated beaches and coves of the island. They needed no one but themselves.

'Why should we want to motor long distances?' she asked him when he tried to make her choose their long-term destination over lunch that first day.

'We have everything we need here on Corfu.' When he wasn't looking she allowed her gaze to dwell on him with open adoration. She had all she needed here, right here within arm's reach. If only he felt the same she would want for nothing more.

He seemed happy to stay near the island too. After lunch he rowed the rubber tender ashore so he could show her the caves they had visited on that ill fated visit long ago.

He was looking incredibly handsome and alert, despite the long sleepless night behind them, and was wearing white shorts and a polo shirt. Their colour gave his burnished skin an added lustre, highlighting the jagged thrust of his cheekbones and the mysterious hollows of his eyes.

In the shadowy cave there was hardly any sound except the bumping of the rubber dinghy against the smooth rocks and the lap-lapping of the water. The walls soared above them in a mixture of blood-red, purple, green and pearl.

This time he had the skill to explain the legend of the caves. 'They are the place of resolutions that cannot be broken, and of meetings for those whose love is undeclared. Listen!'

He whispered something, lifting his dark head to the high roof of the cave. Gentle as a breath came back the shape of her own name on the watery air.

It's only a trick, she told herself as the echo faded. She felt angry at the leap her heart had given, as if in expectation of the sound meaning something.

Christos was watching her, but when she shrugged and began to slither over the rocks away from him he climbed after her, taking the lead out of the dank depths. He seemed jerky and tense, his face white in the gloom, now apparently impatient to be away. She couldn't see his face as he took his seat at the oars of the rubber dinghy. He rowed out of the cave towards the yacht with hard, angry strokes.

That night his lovemaking was as complete as before, but he was unusually silent. No Greek words of love escaped his lips. His eyes brooded over her form in the satin sheets, starlight filtering into the cabin and emptying his face of colour.

They moved out of the natural harbour near Paleokastritsa, motoring down the coast and anchoring off the monastery at Mirtidion.

There, in the courtyard of the village in the early evening, they saw village girls dancing in a ring, their young men taking it in turns to dance in the middle until their fancy was caught by a particular face, then the two would perform a gentle mating dance within the circle of moving figures.

When Christos and she appeared, they were quickly invited into the dance, and Christos took centre floor, head thrown back, a remote expression on his dark face as he held Shelley's glance.

She found herself in the outer circle with the village girls, who swished their full skirts with coquettish grace and stamped out the intricate patterns of the steps, hands on swaying hips, black hair gleaming in the evening sun.

While he danced, Christos's eyes never left her face. She was mesmerised by him, drawn into the dark world behind the façade. Without speaking they seemed to communicate by movement alone, set apart from the rest of the dancers, in a place where there was neither time nor space, just the deep silence of unspoken desire between them.

And then Shelley felt herself being led into the dance by one of the young Greek men. Christos's eyes burned through her skull as the circle of dancers closed round them. The young man spun her this way and that and she lost all sense of where she was, but when they came to a breathless halt Christos had taken the hand of one of the other girls, his hands on the slim waist laced up tightly in the Corfiot dress of black bodice and full skirt worn over layers of multi-coloured petticoats. He was at home, here, she saw. Her eyes followed him possessively while he spun his partner to the clapping of the other dancers.

When he finished his head lifted and his eyes raked the faces of the other dancers until they alighted on Shelley, as if it was a signal to leave. He held her glance, eyes dark and full of meaning. She brushed a hand over her hair, her mouth already burning for his touch.

But another young man appeared, sweeping her with a laugh into his arms, and she found herself back in the middle again. Every time she looked for Christos the dance would separate them, the drums beating faster, the dancers' feet flashing ever quicker, the heat and noise rising to a crescendo. Suddenly he was near her again and she felt her wrist trapped in his hard grasp.

His voice cut sharply through the noise. In English he said, 'This is enough.'

Before she could resist he was dragging her from

the group with a brief comment to the dancers in
Greek.

Saying nothing else, he guided her away from the
square in the direction of the beach. The sound of
the music came to them clearly across the sands.
When they were a little distance away he pulled her
possessively into his arms, lips ranging roughly down
the column of her throat and across the soft skin at
her nape, before softening when he felt her recoil.
'You belong to me. I am a jealous man. Never
forget.'

He pulled her down beside him on to one of the
abandoned sun-beds, and his mouth found hers in
the darkness, his hot breath against her skin. She
slid her hands hungrily inside his shirt. She was back
at once in the mindless happiness of that first night,
shivering as he eased her down on to the gaudy
cushions, white heat igniting at once beneath his
touch.

But suddenly he pulled back, as if remembering
where they were. He folded her impatient hands in
his and whispered, 'Not here; we'll go back to the
yacht. Come!'

Back on board he made love to her in the open on
the sundeck, spreading her naked limbs so that she
lay voluptuously under the stars. His fingers shook
with desire as he undressed her.

'A moon sacrifice for Aphaia,' he murmured,
lifting her limbs in the pale half-light. 'She answered
my prayers, Shelley.' He made love to her with the
first sliver of the new moon hanging like a tinsel
decoration in the inky night.

To Shelley his words seemed to show that his

erotic pleasure in her was unabated, but she tortured herself with the conviction that it went no deeper than desire.

The heavily descending night enveloped them. In a frenzy to melt the ice in his heart, she loved him recklessly, fiercely, passionately, as if tomorrow would never come.

On their last night they sat on deck to watch the last of the sun as it settled over the horizon in a flood of gold. By contrast the sea was like ink. There seemed to be no living soul in the world except themselves. From the radio inside the cabin came the sound of a current hit, the blue notes adding a nostalgic sense of the end of things.

They had got into the habit of preparing meals together in the luxuriously appointed galley, but tonight Christos insisted on doing things himself.

While he was busy Shelley sat on deck and watched the sun slanting across the distant mountains. Soon it would be level with the horizon, and night would come.

The last night of their honeymoon. Then back to the real world. A shudder ran through her. For days now she had staved off the premonition, but now she couldn't fool herself any longer. True, he had revealed a depth of physical passion she had only guessed at. But for the rest. . . She shivered again, not from cold, but from a mixture of memory and fear for their future.

What she knew now beyond any shadow of a doubt was that Christos had never forgotten and never forgiven what had been said to him in the past by both Paula and her father. It had become the spur to an already ambitious nature, the fulcrum for all his subsequent actions.

Marrying Colin Burton's daughter was unarguable proof that he had left behind his past of dishonour and that obscure sense of guilt he felt about his father's death.

Now he was free of it. His absolution was visible, his success obvious. His power was complete.

After dinner they sat under the awning on the aft deck, drowsy and suntanned and to all appearances content. While they drank the last of the wine he took a piece of rope from round one of the stanchions and began to weave the two ends into an intricate knot.

'There,' he said abruptly when he finished. He threw it over to her. 'For you.'

She caught it, touched and surprised at the gesture, wondering what significance it had, if any.

'My thank-you, Shelley,' he said before she could speak. 'You have given me much pleasure in these nights.'

Her eyes dulled and she felt her neck jerk, a spasm of pain making her dip her head, veiling her face beneath her long hair. She didn't need confirmation that she meant nothing deeper than that. She could only fiddle with the sailor's knot he'd tied and give him a stricken little smile.

That night he seemed to make love to her with an extra dimension of passion, driving her to the discovery of a depth of feeling she hadn't known she possessed. Her eyes were moist as she felt his strong

body plunge and relax with shudders of repletion
shaking through him deeper than ever into her core.

When he eventually slept her arms came round to
hold him against her body, fingers splaying across
his rough chest, her face pressing in silence against
the knotted muscles of his back. There was so much
unsaid. And she held him as if it was for the last
time.

With Christos at the wheel they made port just as
the harbour lights were coming on. It was a very
pretty scene, the quayside cafés with their lights and
awnings, people walking up and down in bright
summer clothes, and lights from the villas starring
the hillsides, but Shelley saw everything through a
blur of unhappiness.

The car was already waiting for them at the marina
when they came in. Seeing it, Christos went straight
over to speak to the driver. She saw his face change.
When he returned to make sure everything on the
boat was in order he avoided her glance.

Less than half an hour later they were alighting
from the vehicle outside the villa when she discovered the reason for his odd manner. She had just
started to ascend the steps to the imposing entrance
when she saw a familiar figure through the glass in
the lighted foyer.

She gave a gasp and turned to Christos. His face
showed no element of surprise. He strode the last
few steps to the top to greet the woman who had
come out to meet them. 'Hello, Paula,' he intoned
in the flat, hard tones he adopted to hide his anger.
'Welcome back to Corfu.'

'Christos.' The scarlet lips parted in a tentative smile, and Shelley saw her stepmother's green eyes sweep with sudden approval over the handsome face of her new son-in-law. 'Marriage suits you,' she remarked with a more confident smile. 'It looks as if it suits you very much indeed.'

CHAPTER TEN

PAULA was as couture-thin as ever. Her tan was an expensive shade of gold, and the plunging V of her yellow jacket suggested it was the all-over variety. Her head of cropped black hair was in its usual immaculate condition, and her green eyes were huge and unwavering, as if she couldn't unfix them from Christos's face.

'Hello,' Shelley said incisively, feeling windswept, her presence apparently unnoticed.

'Darling!' Glittering emerald swept at once over her tanned face, and Paula teetered halfway down the steps towards her. When she reached her she gave her a hug. 'I was so worried for you, Shelley,' she husked. 'You gave us so little warning. But I guess that's you Burtons all over.'

Shelley gave her stepmother the obligatory kiss on the cheek, catching sight of Christos over her shoulder. He was standing at the top of the steps and witnessed this reunion with an ironic smile. He looked bronzed and fit after their honeymoon, in white drills, T-shirt and a pair of scuffed white docksiders from off the yacht. She longed to go to him. But she averted her glance.

'Is Dad all right?' she asked with a nervous tremor.

Paula smiled. 'Go in and say hello.'

Shelley's cheeks blanched. 'What? He's here?'

157

Paula nodded.

'But he can't be.' She gazed at her stepmother in dismay before her glance flew back to Christos.

He wore the look of a man in charge of destiny.

Without another word she tore past him, legs a flash of gold beneath her white skirt, but, pushing through the glass doors, she came to an abrupt halt.

'Dad?' Her frightened glance flew over his craggy features.

He came towards her. Then his arms were round her in a strong hug.

'How are you?' she queried, holding him at arm's length to give his face a careful examination.

'I'm as fit as a fiddle.' His pale face and somehow shrunken appearance belied his words. He patted Shelley's hand.

Just then Christos came up, and Shelley swivelled in alarm. She stepped protectively between him and her father.

Christos didn't say anything, but he reached out and put one arm round her waist. He drew her against him as if to stake his claim. She felt like a traitor as her body touched him with a sudden flare of knowing. She sensed what he must be thinking. He was at last face to face with his enemy.

Trembling, she managed to announce, 'You know Christos already.'

She felt his grip tighten on her waist. To her amazement he offered some platitude about the journey. Then to her further amazement he said, 'You are staying here, of course.' It was a statement, not a question.

'We've booked into a hotel in Kassiópi,' replied Colin Burton at once.

'Nonsense,' replied Christos, equally firmly. 'As family, you stay with us.'

Shelley trembled, watching the two men covertly sizing each other up. To her surprise her father simply nodded in agreement. He took a step forward, eyes fixed on Christos's face. 'Things have changed a lot since the last time we met.' His blue eyes calculated the effect of his words. 'We have much to discuss.'

She felt her fingers tighten on Christos's arm. She could feel the tension rippling through him.

He didn't move. Then she heard him say, 'But there is nothing that cannot wait until the morning. Shelley and I have had a long day.' He spoke in a flat tone, and she looked up in relief at this temporary reprieve. There was a rather derisive gleam in his dark eyes.

He was gazing at Colin Burton with something like amazement, taking in the signs of recent illness on his face and the protective way Paula was holding his arm.

Then he swivelled, touching Shelley on the shoulder. 'Offer your parents a drink. I must instruct my staff.'

She knew it was an excuse to leave them together for a few minutes, because there was a perfectly adequate intercom link with staff quarters. But she nodded, nerves wound tight, aware of the danger in the air.

After he left the tension subsided a little, but when Colin turned to his daughter what he saw brought him to her side at once. 'Is he treating you well?'

The warmth of concern in his blue eyes made her defences waver, and for a second she forgot her anxiety about what he might feel about her wedding and longed simply to throw herself into his arms and spill out the whole unhappy truth.

With an effort she kept her expression carefully blank. 'Of course he's treating me well. Why shouldn't he?'

Because her reply sounded more defensive than she'd intended she covered up by going over to the drinks cabinet.

Colin hadn't finished, however. He followed her. 'You look down, somehow.' His eyes were quizzical.

She gave a hasty shrug. Trust Dad to scent something wrong straight away. 'I'm tired. We had a long trip. What are you allowed to drink?' She swiftly changed the subject.

'Just a small brandy for me and the usual for Paula.'

He went on looking at her, and she felt her worries hammering in her head. 'I know you probably think I'm crazy to have married Christos,' she blurted nervously, 'but it's not as if it was a whirlwind romance, as you probably think. We did meet nine years ago.' She found it difficult to go on, but forced herself to ask, 'You don't mind that I've married him?'

'Mind?' He regarded her seriously for a moment. 'I would have liked to give you away at the wedding. I wish you'd waited.'

'But it's Christos,' she insisted. 'I know how you used to feel about him.'

To her surprise and relief he said, 'As long as he takes care of my baby, why should I mind? I hope you'll have a good marriage.'

She was shocked when he said, 'I had him checked out as soon as Paula told me what you'd done.'

'Dad, you didn't!' Her glance flew to his face, but to her confusion he was smiling.

He put up a hand. 'Naturally I was worried. I am your father, after all. I might have had to try and stop it somehow. I know you're of age, but don't forget you're going to be running Burton's by the time you're thirty — if you still want to — and I couldn't let the company go to some playboy who'd squander it all, could I?'

Shelley gave him a searching glance. What had he found out? Did he suspect Christos had an ulterior purpose in marrying her? But no, why should he? He couldn't know how Christos had lured her out to Corfu.

He took a sip from his glass. 'I discovered Christos is a rising star on the international shipping scene. Monasco Mercantile Marine. Very impressive. He's done brilliantly.'

He turned to Paula. 'Remember we saw their logo in Antigua?'

He gave Shelley a rumpled smile. 'Don't look so anxious, darling. I couldn't have arranged it better myself.'

At that moment Christos appeared in the doorway.

'The guest suite is ready when you are,' he

informed them. His black eyes swept the three faces with that arctic expression she knew so well.

Paula rose to her feet. 'Thank you, Christos. That flight seemed endless.'

Colin Burton got up too, though with a little more difficulty. Glancing towards his new son-in-law, he raised both brows, his handsome, craggy face suddenly watchful. 'We need to talk. I hope tomorrow morning will suit you.'

Christos looked remote, the way he did when he was forcing his emotions under control. 'Naturally you will wish to air your views on our marriage. . .' he began.

Shelley held her breath till it hurt. Now it was going to come. He was going to tell her father how and why he had engineered the whole thing.

But Colin was shaking his head. 'It took us by surprise, but then, as Shelley has just pointed out, you had already met.'

He looked from one to the other as he moved with difficulty towards the door. 'No. There is something else we have to discuss. Something of great importance.' His face was lined, and Shelley's heart turned over. He did suspect. She knew it. And for some reason he was trying to keep cool.

Christos was as impassive as before, but she was relieved when, after a glance at her tense expression, he gave a curt nod. 'Tomorrow morning, then.'

Shelley kisssed both parents as they left, then turned to Christos.

He was watching the two figures make their way round the side of the glowing turquoise pool with its underwater lighting, and when the lamps came on in the bungalow opposite he said tensely, 'What do you think he wants to talk about?'

'I don't know. Perhaps he guesses you engineered this marriage.'

They were both stiff now they were alone. That brief flair of intimacy at the start when he had possessively pulled her to his side had made them accomplices for a moment, but now it had died. He gave her a bleak glance. 'He's the type of man who would do the same himself.'

Then he frowned. 'He's aged a lot in nine years. But he's still formidable. No wonder I was impressed by him when I was younger.'

'Were you?' She eyed him in surprise.

Christos gave a grim smile. 'I took him as my role model in those early years. I knew he had started from nothing, like me. I admired him enormously.'

He ignored her dumbfounded expression. 'Paula's as elegant as ever, isn't she?' he went on. 'Quite stunning for her age.'

'I didn't realise you were such a fan of the Burton family.' She gave a shaky laugh and turned away.

As she hadn't stayed at the Villa before it needed Christos to show her where they were going to sleep. She eyed the large double bed in his luxuriously appointed apartment with misgivings.

'Christos,' she began, sure he was going to suggest separate arrangements, and pride forcing her to be the first to suggest it, 'are we both going to sleep here?'

He eyed her in astonishment. 'You are my wife. Where else would you sleep?'

She felt him move towards her with a savage jerk, then pull himself up sharp. His dark eyes pierced hers, but all he said was, 'I'll give you the conducted tour of our living quarters in the morning. You wish to go to sleep straight away?'

She nodded. 'But I'll take a shower first.' Conscious of the way his watchful expression followed her all the way to the bathroom adjoining his bedroom, she pressed the door shut. Then, confused and unhappy, she slipped out of her clothes.

Looking round, she was conscious of his thoughtful preparations for her arrival. There were shelves crammed with bath oils and gels and shampoos in her favourite perfume. A fluffy bathrobe with her initials embroidered on the lapel hung on a peg, and a pair of towelling mules to match were lined up underneath. It was just like Christos to calculate everything to the last perfect detail, she was thinking.

She stepped under the powerful jets and closed her eyes. How on earth was she to survive this marriage, knowing he didn't love her? Now there was the worry of what would happen tomorrow too. Would Christos keep quiet about his reasons for marrying her? She hoped and prayed he would. But why did her father want to have a serious talk with him? It could only be because he suspected something. She trembled. Tempers would surely fly.

Christos, half undressed, broke into her thoughts by yanking open the shower curtain and demanding, 'Are you coming to bed?'

His glance smouldered over her naked body. She turned her back. 'Don't stare at me like that.'

The metal hoops holding the curtain rattled back into place. Relieved to escape his lingering inspection, she slicked shower gel over her breasts and thighs, giving herself briefly to the sensual pleasure of the perfume that enveloped her. Then she gave a gasp.

The curtain had rattled back again and the hard, familiar body of her husband moulded itself to her own. Water cascaded over both of them, but he seemed unaware of it. His arms came right round her waist and gripped her in a possessive embrace against his hard shape.

When she wriggled he turned her round and began to nuzzle hungrily against her throat.

'Don't dare try to dismiss me like that,' he rasped. 'You are still my wife.'

Her fingers grappled at his rapidly soaking T-shirt, and she gasped as his lips traced a burning trail down to the hollow between her breasts.

He pressed even closer, his voice thickening with desire. 'You are the most beautiful woman in the world. I want you. Come.'

Lances of spray glanced off the bones of his cheeks and nose, blinding her as his hot mouth claimed hers in a swoop of possession. Gasping, she tried to struggle from his grasp, but already she was melting beneath his touch. The power jets drenched them both, her face tilted, his wet head raining more water over her. She shut her eyes, lids dropping languorously, wet lashes feathering her cheeks, her soft lips opening hungrily to receive his kisses.

She became a being of pure sensation as his

embrace became more passionate and she forgot all her reservations. Nothing mattered but loving him.

His intentions quickly became obvious. He arched her against him. She felt a spasm of yearning for him, and it was like fate driving them both on, showing there was no way she would ever resist him.

'Yes, you want me,' he said in triumph when he witnessed her ardent response. 'Your body cannot lie to me.'

Somehow she was crying his name in affirmation, her own demands matching his as she clung to his strong body, fingers clawing beneath the wet T-shirt to caress the knotted muscles of his back. The jets flung water over their one form in an enveloping cascade, enclosing them in a private domain where nothing existed but the depth of mutual desire. A blurred image of a sculpture, two lovers in one of the Athenian fountains, came to mind, making her wish they could be like that, like a stone image, held in an embrace time could not destroy.

Then beneath his sure touch all images surrendered to the shuddering tides of sensation that swept through her with every powerful thrust of possession. He called her name, a hoarse cry of desire, and everything turned to flame as the tension uncoiled in an explosion of white heat.

The water slowed to a caress over the sensitive planes and hollows of their skin before it trickled to a stop. Steam drifted around them, condensing in shiny beads across his brow. They ran in silver trails down the side of his chiselled jaw. She pressed her moist lips against his wet shoulder, licking it with the tip of her tongue, reluctant to allow him to leave her. Signs of separation were already wrenching them apart, and reality came crowding back.

In the echoing silence when the water stopped Christos went on holding her, arms wrapping tightly round her soft form. His handsome face wore a dazed expression, as if he was unable to believe he was standing under the shower with Shelley in his arms.

Slowly recovering, he growled at last, 'What did you do?' He looked angry for a moment. 'You wanted me just as much,' he announced, as if defending himself against an unspoken accusation.

When she didn't reply he said curtly, 'Come to bed.'

He stripped off his wet T-shirt. Wrapping her in a large towel, he made her stand on the tiles in the middle of the bathroom and began to pat her dry all over. He lifted each limb with tender care, then rubbed her long hair until it was almost dry too.

She stood still and allowed him to complete this process while her thoughts ranged shakily over the last few minutes. How could she feel so in love with a man who had married her for all the wrong reasons, whose only feeling was one of driving desire?

It was madness, but her love held firm when all sense told her to give up on it.

He peered carefully into her eyes when she was dry, but with an abrupt change he reached for another towel and began to dry himself.

'Get into bed,' he told her.

A few seconds later the mattress indented as he climbed in beside her. She turned on her side, away

from him, and felt him curve his body round her
own. One of his hands slid into the roots of her hair
and the other cupped one of her breasts.

In a few moments his fingers stilled and she could
feel his breath, warm and even against her shoulder,
and she knew he was asleep.

She lay like that for some time, sheltered within
his sleeping shape, listening to him breathe, her
heart aching.

Next morning Shelley had a late breakfast beside the
pool. Christos had got up while she still slept, and
now he was in his office with her father, deep in
discussion, and she expected to hear raised voices at
any moment.

Her glance kept straying to the open picture
window, where they were clearly visisble.

Paula came out and sat down under a blue parasol.
Her glance followed Shelley's.

'Colin is showing Christos his plans for another
hotel down the coast,' she remarked.

Surprised, Shelley found her expectation of
trouble only intensified. 'What on earth is he doing
that for?'

'Well, I suppose he sees Christos as the heir
apparent to the Burton throne. Or perhaps one
should say the prince regent?' Before Shelley could
ask her what she meant she went on, 'You still hope
to carry on now you're married, I suppose.'

Dully Shelley nodded. What had this to do with
Paula? She wasn't interested in the company. 'What
else are they discussing, do you know?'

'Haven't a clue,' replied Paula airily. 'Boring business, I expect; you know your father.'

She came to sit at the smart white table next to Shelley and helped herself to a cup of coffee. 'Colin thinks Christos made a very smart move, marrying you, my dear. It meant he acquired a considerable property empire to add to his shipping interests in one neat act.'

Shelley's cup jerked to a stop halfway to her lips. There was no need for Paula to kick her when she was already down.

But her stepmother had tilted her sunglasses and was regarding Shelley quizzically from over the top. 'I admit our first thought was he'd probably steam-rollered you into marriage when he saw what was at stake——'

'I don't want to hear this,' muttered Shelley.

'Oh, but you should,' Paula continued, 'because last night after I'd seen you both together I told your father not to be such a buffoon.' She let her glasses drop back into place. 'Christos and I had a long talk this morning before you were up.'

'You and Christos?' Shelley drained her coffee-cup and reached for the pot again.

'He was very forthright and put me straight on one or two things.'

'He did? I can't imagine what.'

'Well, for one thing, he told me about what happened, or in fact didn't happen, that night all those years ago.'

Her voice changed. 'I am sorry, Shelley. I didn't behave well. I misjudged you, and I misjudged him too if it comes to that. I was only trying to protect you.'

'Of course you were.' She couldn't restrain the note of bitter irony in her tone.

Paula sat up straight. Her voice gave a slight wobble. 'You never really gave me a chance, you know. I hoped, in time, we could at least be friends.'

She seemed to brace herself. 'You always fought me. But you've got to hear this. That summer when we were over here, it was only my second year with your father. I was still measuring myself against your mother, aware that I would never be as good as she was. I was desperately afraid of losing him. I didn't see what he could find in me to hold his interest. And then there was you.'

She frowed and leaned forward. 'You were such a beautiful child, and that summer I saw you changing before my eyes into a beautiful young woman. Suddenly all the looks were for you. It frightened me. Can you understand that? I realised what a responsibility I now had. I've never been the mothering type. I'm too frivolous. But here was this beautiful child I had to protect.'

Shelley was still dwelling on the image of Paula and Christos having a talk. It sent tremors of anxiety up and down her body. What else had he told her?

Paula reached over and gripped her by both shoulders. 'You're not listening to me, Shelley! Hear what I'm saying! Please! I'm saying I'm sorry for reacting the way I did. I know it made matters worse.'

Shelley's bottom lip trembled and she said, 'You

only did what any mother would have done. It would have turned out the way it has anyway.'

Paula took off her sunglasses and fiddled with them, different expressions chasing themselves across her face.

'I shouted all those dreadful things at Christos. I completely lost control.'

She coloured slightly. 'I thought he had talked you into making love. I didn't see how any girl could resist him if he set his mind to seducing them. He was — is,' she corrected, 'such a breathtakingly handsome man, funny and kind and generous too, all of it apparent even at twenty. I knew he must have plenty of girls at his feet.' She reached out. 'I didn't realise how sincere his feelings were. I never meant to destroy things for you.'

Suddenly her arms were round Shelley. 'Say you forgive me for being so dreadful, darling.'

Shelley tried to smile. 'You didn't destroy anything, Paula. There was nothing to destroy.'

'Nothing?' Paula looked puzzled. 'Christos was besotted by you. Don't you remember how he couldn't keep away for a minute? But we were happy you had someone near your own age to go around with, and until you stayed out that night we felt we could trust him.'

'You needn't have worried,' replied Shelley bitterly. 'He wasn't besotted as you think. He simply saw himself as the prince rescuing the poor little rich girl from loneliness. And that night, as I'm sure he told you, he behaved like a gentleman.' She felt tears crowd irrationally behind her eyes.

Paula touched her arm. 'My dear, I promise I

won't interfere, but it's obvious there's something terribly wrong. Why don't you talk to him. . .? You mustn't hurt him, Shelley. He's very special.'

Shelley drew back, wiping the back of one hand over her eyes. 'I know you mean well, Paula, but you don't know the truth. You were close to it when you said he'd steamrollered me into marriage.' Her eyes were swimming. 'I don't know what story he's told you about the past, but, if it's what I think it is, it really isn't true.'

Paula didn't ask her what she meant, because at that moment Christos himself came walking round the side of the pool towards them. She leaned across the table. 'Go to him, my dear. Talk to him,' she murmured hurriedly. 'Don't let it die.'

When Shelley turned, Christos's glance found hers at once. She felt Paula get up and walk away. Then Christos came to the table and sat down and poured himself a cup of coffee. They were alone.

'Why don't you talk to him?' Paula had suggested. But what was the point? He didn't love her, and no amount of talking about it would change that.

A hurried glance over her shoulder revealed her father strolling amiably out through the doors of the office. She saw him give Paula a contented smile and, looping one arm in hers, proceed to amble towards one of the terraces on the other side of the villa.

So Christos hadn't told him the truth. She breathed a sigh of relief.

Turning to Christos, she managed, 'I hope you'll never tell Dad why you engineered this marriage. It would kill him.'

He gazed remotely into her eyes. 'Of course I would tell him if he asked, but I imagine he's capable of working it out for himself.'

'I hope not. He'd go mad.'

'Why should he? We get on well. I think he likes me.' He gave a bitter smile.

He regarded her from across the table. 'He's looking for somebody to take over the running of Burton's. He feels it's time he retired. This last illness shook him up. He thinks you're still too young. He wants somebody to run it for the next few years so that when you're ready you can take over.'

'Aren't you in luck?' she heard herself say in bitter tones. 'You have everything you want.'

'I wish I had.'

There was a note of such unhappiness in his voice that her head jerked up. 'Haven't you? You've got everything you set your heart on. You've got your good name back. And now you've got a property empire as well.'

He gave a growl of anger, and she felt his hand shoot out and pin her arm to the table. 'I've got my name, yes. I've got you, yes. And I've got a string of successful companies and everything money can buy. But the most important thing is missing.'

He brought a hand up and ran it savagely through her hair, his fingers softening almost at once and completing the gesture with a slow sensuality, his black eyes burning into her upturned face with open desire.

'What's missing?' she asked shakily. She felt she had to hear him say it.

Her worst fears were confirmed when he gave that brief jerk of the head she knew so well. 'Love,' he said harshly. 'Love is missing. The one thing that makes it all worth while.'

'But you knew that!' the words wrenched from deep inside her. 'Why did you insist on going on with it?'

His face was grey. 'I thought once you were back here on Corfu things would be different. But from that first moment when you came in through the doors into the office I knew you hated me. Then, instead of taking things slowly, I rushed you into marriage. I thought a ring—the Kiriakis ring— would work its magic, and you would remember how it had once been between us.' He shrugged and his lips twisted with bitterness.

'But I didn't hate you,' she managed, not sure what he was saying, only desperate to put the record straight. 'I was frightened by what you made me feel.'

She reached out blindly, desperate to touch him, to feel his warm skin beneath her fingertips. 'I don't care if you married me just to restore your honour and make your mother happy in her old age. I don't care any more, Christos, don't you see that?'

He gripped her fiercely by the shoulders, his face twisting in an agony of emotion. 'What do you mean?'

She gazed at him for a long, dragging moment then whispered, 'I love you. I love you so much. I always have. You must know that. I couldn't do the things we do in bed if I didn't. I'll try to live with this feeling, but I must tell you, it kills me to know you only want me to right a wrong.'

Her soft lips trembled. Now her pride was in tatters, but somehow it didn't matter. Nothing mattered except loving him.

She felt him reach out and draw her into his embrace. 'What did you say? Say it again.' His lips rested against the side of her head. 'Shelley. Tell me again what you said just now.'

She felt her eyes fill and through her lashes she saw the front of his shirt moisten. 'I said I love you, Christos. I love you so much. It hurts; I don't know how to live with it.'

His grip tightened and he was squeezing her so hard that she could scarcely breathe. 'But you said you didn't want marriage without love.' He broke off and held her so he could examine her expression. 'I thought you meant you didn't love me.'

'Just the opposite,' she managed, blue eyes swimming. 'I know *you* don't love *me*. I knew it would be hell on earth to be married to you, knowing that. I dreaded it so much.'

'But why do you imagine I plotted to bring you to my side? I've been driven by the desire to make you my wife ever since that long-ago summer. Everything I've ever done has been for you.'

'But Christos. . .' She lifted a hand and touched the warm skin in the V of his shirt as if she had never touched him before. 'I thought you blamed me for what happened between you and your father. I thought you felt so dishonoured by what was said to you that all you wanted was revenge.'

'You think that was the only reason I wanted to

marry you?' He crushed her hard against his chest in a spasm of emotion. 'Shelley, I never blamed you for what happened between Father and myself. We always had a fiery relationship, though I admit I felt guilty at the fact that we never made our peace.'

He brushed her forehead with his lips and was holding her tight, as if he thought she might escape at any moment. He continued, 'I was furious at being publicly and wrongly accused, but now I understand why you were silent that day; you expected me to speak out in our defence, but I was too young and proud to do so. Perhaps when we have daughters of our own I shall understand your father's anger.'

His dark eyes flamed over her face and his voice throbbed with emotion. 'Shelley, I love you. For nine long years you have been my guiding star.'

Shelley reached out to him and Christos held her close, fingers running over and over through her hair. 'I can't quite believe this all at once,' she whispered.

He smoothed her hair. 'I longed to touch you like this nine years ago, but forced myself to behave correctly because I felt I hadn't got the right.'

He brought one of the golden strands to his lips. It was the fulfilment of all her dreams to hear him say he loved her and had always loved her. It made her more happy than she would ever have believed.

'I fell in love with you from that first moment our eyes met. I'd never seen anyone like you. You were a Greek pirate and you stole my heart.'

He started to lead her to a secluded lawn at the back of the villa. When they reached a sheltered spot he pulled her down into the grass. She lay back in his arms.

He examined the expression on her face, and the edges of his mouth began to lift. 'You are so beautiful, Shelley, even more beautiful than you were at sixteen. When I saw you in the garden with Spyro's children it was a revelation. I had thought of you till then as Aphrodite, goddess of love, but then I saw you as the mother of my children. It was a strange feeling. It shook through me with such power.'

He lay back in the grass and pulled her on top of him. 'It's very secluded here,' he pointed out.

'So?' she queried softly.

He lifted his black brows and gave her one of his heart-stopping smiles.

Without speaking, she began to unbutton his shirt. 'It was you who told me the story of the Illyrian princess,' she warned in a husky voice. 'Would you like me to follow her example?'

He lay back, a smile playing round his lips. 'Yes, my dear wife, do whatever you please. I am entirely in your hands.' He closed his eyes.

She finished unbuttoning his shirt, placing a kiss on each inch of his bronzed torso as it was revealed. Then she reached for the buckle on his belt, and soon she was showing him exactly what she wanted, until it became difficult to tell who was making the decisions, because their movements melted into one and became a single flowing river of love and desire.

Welcome to Europe

CORFU — 'the garden isle of Greece'

Floating in the Ionian Sea, and generally acknowledged to be the island used by Shakespeare as the setting for his play, *The Tempest*, Corfu is greener than many other Greek islands because of its higher level of winter rainfall. It is known as 'the garden isle', and if you visit it in spring you will be bound to see why. A carpet of wild flowers covers the slopes of the island — the whites and golds of marigolds, camomiles and crown daisies in February and March lead into a profusion of contrasting scarlet, pink and purple in April and May with the poppies, wild geraniums and gladioli. The perfect place for a spring honeymoon!

THE ROMANTIC PAST

Corfu's first recorded history begins in 734 BC, with the foundation of a colony from Corinth. Then called **Corcyra**, a name also given to the main town, in 330 AD the island became part of the Byzantine Empire, and in the sixth century AD the population resettled on the promontory, site of the present Old Fort, naming the new town **Korifo**, from the word *korifai*, meaning 'twin peaks'.

The present name, **Corfu**, is an Italianised version of Korifo, but the Greeks still call their island and the town **Kérkira**. This name may be mythical—Corcyra was the mistress of the sea god Poseidon. It was their offspring, Phaiax, who gave his name in turn to the mythical people, the **Phaeacians**, who according to Homer in *The Odyssey* inhabited the island. On the other hand, the name Kérkira may be geographical, originating from the Greek word *kerkos* meaning 'tail' or 'handle', referring to its shape. Even more confusingly, when Homer referred to Corfu he gave it the name of **Scheria**!

Four centuries of Venetian rule, followed by the French and British, gave Corfu a legacy of fine but surprisingly un-Greek architecture. The tall, narrow buildings and little squares come from the Venetians, but the arcades on the Esplanade in Corfu Town are most definitely reminiscent of Paris's rue de Rivoli. And the period of British rule from 1814 to 1864 has given to the island apple chutney, *kek* (rich fruit cake), *tsintsin bira* (ginger beer) and cricket!

In the lagoon of Chalikiopoulos, south of Corfu Town, is the little island of **Pondikonisi**—Mouse Island. Legend says that this used to be the ship taking Odysseus home from Troy to Ithaca after his travels. Having just escaped the clutches of Calypso, **Odysseus** was deposited naked on a Corfu beach — no one can prove exactly where, but Ermones and Paleokastritsa are likely candidates — and rescued by **Nausicaa**, daughter of Alcinous, king of the Phaeacians, who had come with her women to wash the household linen. He was so handsome that she knew he had to be a prince or a god, and she persuaded her father to give him a ship to take him home. But Poseidon was angry at Odysseus' escape, and turned the ship into stone.

In recent centuries it has been the events of the Greek orthodox calendar which have provided a basis for the Corfiot people to gather and feast. In Corfu Town there are four processions in honour of the patron saint, **St Spiridon**; the most spectacular of these is at Easter. After parades and processions, the Corfiots find a release for their emotions in the ritual of the **breaking of the pots**. At eleven o'clock sharp, wine jars, flower pots and cheap crockery come crashing down into the street below, thrown from balconies and windows. This is a symbolic ritual going back many centuries; its meaning is obscure, but one theory suggests it represents the stoning of Judas. With its protective arcades, Nikiforos Theotakis Street is a good place to watch the spectacle — but don't step out until you're sure the last pot has been launched!

Many famous people have lived and worked in Corfu: **Edward Lear**, who said that the island made him 'grow younger every hour'; **Henry Miller**;

Evelyn Waugh, who wrote that Corfu Town reminded him of Brighton; the writer **Lawrence Durrell**, and his younger brother **Gerald Durrell**, whose three boyhood years on the island were the basis for his book *My Family and Other Animals*.

THE ROMANTIC PRESENT — pastimes for lovers. . .

Corfu is an island with lots to see and do, but it's probably best to start off with Corfu Town itself, just to get a flavour of the contrasts and history of the island.

Tourism is one of Corfu's main industries, so in July and August expect the town to be quite busy! It's a good place to use as a base, but, if you're just spending a day there, start your explorations in the **Esplanade** or Spianada, which is one of Europe's largest squares. Stroll along the west side of the square, where the French-style arcades, known as the **Liston**, house restaurants, cafés, tea rooms and bookshops, and then visit the little streets behind for some serious shopping. Here you will also come across the sixteenth-century church of **St Spiridon**, the patron saint of Corfu, said to have saved the town from famine, plague, the Turks and Second World War bombs. Half the male population of Corfu has the name Spiros or Spyros!

North-east of these is the **Campiello**, the Old Town, a densely built and crumbling maze of narrow lanes, twisting alleys, steps, and some of the finest examples of Venetian brick and stucco architecture. These houses are in contrast to the stone-built neo-classical buildings of the British colonial period, such as the **Palace of St Michael and St George** at the north end of the Esplanade, which was the former residence of the British Lord High Commissioner.

There are two other very interesting buildings near to Corfu Town. Just to the south is **Mon Repos**, a villa set in parkland which was built in 1824 for Sir Frederick Adam, then given to the Greek royal family; Prince Philip, Duke of Edinburgh, was born here in 1921. And a little further away is the **Achilleion**, a pleasure palace built for the Empress Elisabeth of Austria in 1888–91. It is a fanciful re-creation of a Phaeacian palace of legend, set in a wooded landscape and dedicated to Achilles, a Greek hero who fascinated the Empress. It's open to the public and in summer is now used as a casino; the James Bond film *For Your Eyes Only* was filmed in its gardens.

If you feel the need to get out of town, you could continue south from Corfu Town on the coast road, past Benitses to reach the southern end of the island at Kavos. On the way, make sure you don't miss a left-hand turn into the hills at the small hamlet of Linia; this leads you to the charming hill village of **Chlomos**, which was visited — and painted — by Edward Lear. Then take a westerly return route and see the thirteenth-century **Castle of Gardiki**. On another day you could go to **Kassiópi** on the northeastern coast. A historic early settlement with a Venetian castle on its headland, this is now a picturesque fishing village, developed for tourism but still attractive and atmospheric.

By the time you return from your excursions to Corfu Town you will be just in time to catch the **Volta**, the traditional ritual evening stroll around the town square. Everyone comes out for this, dressed in their best clothes, and, as you can imagine, it is a good opportunity for marriageable girls to spot likely husbands!

There is certainly no lack of choice of eating places in Corfu. The essential ingredients of Greek cooking are olive oil, garlic, lemon, and herbs such as thyme, oregano, mint, fennel, rosemary and sage, gathered wild on the slopes of the hills; so try meat, fish or vegetable dishes with local sauces like **skordalia**, a garlic and potato paste, or **avgolemono**, an egg and lemon sauce added to soups or casseroles.

You will find pasta dishes, called **makaronia**—it was via the Ionian islands that the Venetians introduced the rest of Greece to pasta. Generally it is used as an accompaniment to meat, or baked with minced meat in a pie, a dish which is called **pastitsio**. The Greeks are also great bean eaters and have a passion for **fasolia soupa** (white bean soup). Common too are **yemista** or stuffed vegetables—tomatoes, peppers or aubergines stuffed with mince, onions and rice, or with pine nuts, raisins and feta cheese. And two specialities particular to Corfu are **veal sofrito**, a beef stew, and **bourdetto**, a white fish stew.

For dessert, you must try the wild strawberry (**fraoula**), in season between April and June. And those with a sweet tooth should also look out for **glika koutaliou** ('spoon sweets'), which are fruits crystallised in a sugar syrup—on Corfu particularly the kumquat.

Finally, you're bound to want to take home a **souvenir** of your holiday, or presents for friends and family. Corfiot olive oil is wonderfully green and smooth and redolant of summer days, as is the local orange liqueur. Sponges and leather goods, Minoan-style jewellery and carved olive wood ornaments and utensils are among the local specialities. The most sophisticated shops in Corfu Town are in Voulgareos Street, but the best area for crafts is the labyrinth of streets to the south of the port. We're sure you won't be short of choice!

DID YOU KNOW THAT. . .?

* Corfu is the only Greek island with a **cricket field**—the islanders' pleasure in the game is a legacy of the period of British rule.

* The island's main **exports** are wine, fish, and olive oil. In the early years of their occupation the Venetians offered Corfiot landowners special cash benefits for the planting of olive trees.

* Over 17% of the island's agricultural area is devoted to vine cultivation.

* The currency of Greece is the **drachma**.

* To say 'I love you' in Greek, you murmur '*S'agapo*' in your beloved's ear. Or, if you want to be a little more direct, you could try, '*Dose mou ena phili*' — 'Give me a kiss'!

**LOOK OUT FOR TWO TITLES EVERY
MONTH IN OUR SERIES OF
EUROPEAN ROMANCES:**

ICE AT HEART: Sophie Weston (Sweden)
Gaby's father's reputation was at stake, so she was
forced to help Dr Sven Hedberg. But she hadn't
counted on the magnetic attraction between
them. . .

DARK SIDE OF THE ISLAND: Edwina Shore
(Barra — Outer Hebrides)
Briony was back on the Hebridean island of Barra,
and under Kyle's roof again, where he surely didn't
want her, any more than she wanted to be there. . .

DANGEROUS DESIRE: Sarah Holland (Monaco)
Isabelle adored Monaco — but hated Jean-Luc. But
he *was* incredibly handsome, and seemed to want to
help. Could she trust him?

BITTER MEMORIES: Margaret Mayo (Tenerife)
Tanya was shocked to bump into Alejandro Vazquez
Herrera the moment she arrived in Tenerife — she
hadn't expected ever to see him again. Could she
resist him second time around?

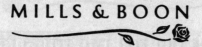

MILLS & BOON

Proudly present...

CHARLOTTE LAMB'S

♥ 100th ♥

ROMANCE

This is a remarkable achievement for a writer who had her first Mills & Boon novel published in 1973. Some six million words later and with sales around the world, her novels continue to be popular with romance fans everywhere.

Her centenary romance '*VAMPIRE LOVER*' is a suspense-filled story of dark desires and tangled emotions—Charlotte Lamb at her very best.

Published: June 1994   **Price:** £1.90

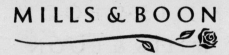

MILLS & BOON

HEARTS OF FIRE by Miranda Lee

Welcome to our compelling family saga set in the glamorous world of opal dealing in Australia. Laden with dark secrets, forbidden desires and scandalous discoveries, **Hearts of Fire** unfolds over a series of 6 books, but each book also features a passionate romance with a happy ending and can be read independently.

Book 1: SEDUCTION & SACRIFICE
Published: April 1994   *FREE* with Book 2

Lenore had loved Zachary Marsden secretly for years. Loyal, handsome and protective, Zachary was the perfect husband. Only Zachary would never leave his wife…would he?

WATCH OUT for special promotions!

Book 2: DESIRE & DECEPTION
Published: April 1994   Price £2.50

Jade had a name for Kyle Armstrong: *Mr Cool*. He was the new marketing manager at Whitmore Opals—the job *she* coveted. However, the more she tried to hate this usurper, the more she found him attractive…

Book 3: PASSION & THE PAST
Published: May 1994   Price £2.50

Melanie was intensely attracted to Royce Grantham—which shocked her! She'd been so sure after the tragic end of her marriage that she would never feel for any man again. How strong was her resolve not to repeat past mistakes?

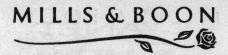

MILLS & BOON

HEARTS OF FIRE by Miranda Lee

Book 4: FANTASIES & THE FUTURE
Published: June 1994   Price £2.50

The man who came to mow the lawns was more stunning than any of Ava's fantasies, though she realised that Vincent Morelli thought she was just another rich, lonely housewife looking for excitement! But, Ava knew that her narrow, boring existence was gone forever…

Book 5: SCANDALS & SECRETS
Published: July 1994   Price £2.50

Celeste Campbell had lived on her hatred of Byron Whitmore for twenty years. Revenge was sweet…until news reached her that Byron was considering remarriage. Suddenly she found she could no longer deny all those long-buried feelings for him…

Book 6: MARRIAGE & MIRACLES
Published: August 1994   Price £2.50

Gemma's relationship with Nathan was in tatters, but her love for him remained intact—she was going to win him back! Gemma knew that Nathan's terrible past had turned his heart to stone, and she was asking for a miracle. But it was possible that one could happen, wasn't it?

Don't miss all six books!

HEART  HEART

Win a year's supply of Romances
<u>ABSOLUTELY</u> FREE?

Yes, you can win one whole year's supply of Mills & Boon Romances. It's easy! Find a path through the maze, starting at the top left square and finishing at the bottom right.
The symbols must follow the sequence above.
You can move up, down, left, right and diagonally.

Please turn over for entry details

HEART ♡ HEART

SEND YOUR ENTRY NOW!

The first five correct entries picked out of the bag after the closing date will each win one year's supply of Mills & Boon Romances (six books every month for twelve months - worth over £85).
What could be easier?

Don't forget to enter your name and address in the space below then put this page in an envelope and post it today (you don't need a stamp).
Competition closes 31st November 1994.

HEART TO HEART Competition
FREEPOST
P.O. Box 236
Croydon
Surrey CR9 9EL

Are you a Reader Service subscriber?   Yes ☐   No ☐

Ms/Mrs/Miss/Mr _____ COMHH

Address _____

_____

_____

_____ Postcode _____

Signature _____

One application per household. Offer valid only in U.K. and Eire. You may be mailed with offers from other reputable companies as a result of this application. Please tick box if you would prefer not to receive such offers. ☐